The views and opinions expressed herein are solely those of the author and do not represent the views and opinions of Idea Machine Output, LLC.

HOUSE OF BOXES

a play in four acts

by Doctor Circus

An Idea Machine Output Publication

Published in 2018 by Idea Machine Output LLC

Cover designed by Leah Odom under strict instruction by Doctor Circus

ISBN: 1-947831-01-1
ISBN-13: 978-1-947831-01-8
LCN: 2017953301

To:
Moira & Aoife
my muses, my hearts
where have you gone?

HOUSE OF BOXES was first presented on October 11th, 1968 in the Maison de Boison auditorium in a location that all parties (except for the author, who is being very kind by omitting it) wish to remain left out of the annuals of history. It was directed by the ingenious Doctor Circus; set and costume were done by the innovative Doctor Circus; lighting was done by the intelligent Doctor Circus; music was lovingly composed by the inventive Doctor Circus. The cast in order of appearance was as follows:

Doctor Circus	Himself
Person from the Audience	A Random Person (who, for legal reasons, shall not be named)
Glee, The Woeful	Samantha Julian
Woe, The Gleeful	Desmond Mohr
John	Robert Mueller
Jane (before the incident)	Luella Stephens
Jane (after the incident)	Marisa Graves
Stagehands	They were too various to name when the first draft was performed.

HOUSE OF BOXES premiered in the Americas under the same circumstances as previously mentioned, except it was in 1995, on June 16th. The cast was different, and was as follows:

Doctor Circus	Himself, there can be no one else
Person from the Audience	Carol Anne Sheppard
Glee, The Woeful	Eliza Morales
Woe, The Gleeful	Marcus Castillo
Actor Playing "John"	Robert Mueller
Actress Playing "Jane" 1	Marisa Graves
Actress Playing "Jane" 2	Teresa Gonzalez
Stagehands	Alejandro Cardenas
	Lucien Acosta
	Carlos Oviedo
	Marcus Rivas

WITHIN THESE PAGES

DRAMATIS PERSONAE

DOCTOR CIRCUS (M)

A very, very handsome man. He is as attractive as he is innovatory. His beard is supreme and is the rival of all men. His clothes are undeniably perfect and clean, that is why they look old and worn. They are the best clothes, so why should the best man on this planet and others, confine himself to any other such attire? It would be foolish to assume he would be wearing anything else than what he would feel comfortable in. He is a true god among men, and everyone should know this.

PERSON FROM THE AUDIENCE (M/F)

Should appear as though they are a random person in the audience, like the first time this historical play was ever unleashed upon the world.

GLEE, THE WOEFUL (F)

The sad jester of the Circus household and the identical sister to Woe, The Gleeful. She, much like everything in The House of Boxes, is positively twisted and wicked and is wrought with sorrow.

WOE, THE GLEEFUL (M)

The happy jester of the Circus household and the identical brother to Glee, The Woeful. He, much like everything in The House of Boxes, is positively twisted and wicked and is wrought with glee.

ACTOR PLAYING "JOHN" (M)

As always, a plain and stiff actor who seems out of place and is acting as though all of his actions have been strictly planned out by the director.

ACTRESS PLAYING "JANE" 1 (F)

A plain and ordinary girl who is scared out of her wits (and rightly so, for she knows what is to come).

ACTRESS PLAYING "JANE" 2 (F)

A slightly less plain and ordinary girl than the girl that played JANE 1. She should be far more afraid, however, for she always has less talent.

STAGEHANDS (Ms)

Strong, muscular stagehands.

1

SETTING

As should be apparent, the main setting of House of Boxes is, in fact, the theatre in which the play is performed. The theatre must have an eerie feel about it and for all intents and purposes must seem completely unwelcoming (much like the human soul). Anyone who enters must immediately feel out of place and as though they must leave for some reason, yet it must feel like they should stay.

On the stage, everything will look very simple, if not Shakespearean (i.e. the forest will be represented by just a cutout tree, or even just some branches taken from a local park, or a disingenuous neighbor who needs to learn a lesson about keeping their business to themselves), yet very complicated (i.e. there should be a real car front for the opening scene). This is to garner some sort of mystique, as though one is trying to seem like they have a bigger budget than they do. [It should be noted, here, that there will be some pretentious critic that may point this out, but you can take solace in the fact that it had been planned all along. If you can't, enjoy the knowledge that they will get what it is coming to them, whether it be a slow death or a quick, quiet jab with the sharpest of knives that has been painstakingly sharpened on many a sleepless night.]

The main set (the "House of Boxes", as it were, itself) should be simple and easy to move on and off the stage. It should be suggested that the main concept of the setting be displayed by rather lavish backdrops, as opposed to large set pieces, so that they can be pulled up or drawn out as the scenes progress. There should also be stacks of wooden boxes scattered around. It might be easiest to put said boxes on wheels (although these practices have never before been put in place). The boxes themselves should have raw meat in them so that the smell can intensify as the show progresses under the strong lights.

There also needs to be a moveable mantle place for the living area, which has a large portrait of Doctor Circus on it. The bedroom should be nothing more than two cots. The dining area should be an elaborate table, but with cheap chairs (because who can afford nice chairs?). There should also be an assorted amount of mannequins scattered throughout the audience (it is important for the audience to know that you don't need them).

LIGHTING

Let's not kid ourselves, lighting is not important for this work in the slightest. The importance of this piece relies on the words that have been written (and should be said verbatim). The work lights, as well as the stage lights, should always be on. Needless lawsuits from those who trip and fall on sharp knives that have been tirelessly sharpened should not be a concern of those putting on a production of this masterpiece. The houselights, however, should be turned all the way down as soon as the show begins (near the end of Rant I), as though it were on a switch.

STYLE

As with all shows before, in an ideal world, those people playing the "Actors" should be played by people who were just pulled off the streets, on a cold night, when desperation is all that can keep one warm. If this is not possible, then actors who can manifest this feeling inside of them should be hired to play those parts.

As it pertains to Doctor Circus, it should be noted that if the lucky person who plays him truly embodies such an impeccable soul, he should be allowed to make impromptu remarks. He is the only one allowed to go "off-book". He can break "the forth wall" as he sees fit. That is to say, he should only do this if he is truly channeling the spirit of the indefectible Doctor Circus. If he is not this caliber, or "up to snuff" as the kids say today, then he should get the fuck off the stage and go grovel at the feet of some other producer that can give him a part that only demands that he cries on command like the whelp that he is.

A NOTE TO WHO PLAYS DOCTOR CIRCUS

As was stated previously (read "Style" above, you fucking direction-seeking actor), if you don't think that you can bring the certain gravitas that is absolutely and unequivocally necessary to embody the author, in his grace and humbleness, Doctor Circus, then you should give this part to someone else. It is known that it is the best part that has ever been bestowed upon you, but if you are unfit (and you should be able to tell if you are unfit, even if you are a cheap lobotomy survivor), then you should make way for someone who is more proper in fitting the shoes of the impervious Doctor Circus.

HOUSE OF BOXES

RANT I

Upon the opening of the doors [30 minutes before showtime] the audience will see DOCTOR CIRCUS sitting CS, in a CHAIR with a CANE in his hand. There's a near-dim spotlight on him, so that he is more illuminated than the rest of the stage. He sits there as though he might be slumbering, making no note of the audience before him. Once it's time for the show to begin, he stirs, rapidly, as though a nightmare that he has experienced infinite times before has befallen him. He seems (but is not) surprised by the audience. But, then, remembrance washes over him.

DOCTOR CIRCUS: *(to the audience, obviously)* Oh, is it about that time already? *(he looks down at his wrist, which, as always, is watch-less)* Well so it is! *(he stands, arms outstretched as though he is greeting the audience as a whole)* Good evening, my fine people. Well aren't you all just lovely? *(he laughs at this for some unknown reason and then looks OS as he speaks)* Why yes you all are. Is everyone seated? *(he gets a nod of approval from some unseen individual, then looks back to the audience with a devilish smile)* Good. *(he stomps his cane down and drops the bullshit "nice host" demeanor instantaneously)* CLOSE THE DOORS! *(he laughs maniacally as the doors CLOSE AND LOCK LOUDLY)* So let us begin. *(he approaches the audience and crouches down as though they are children)* Now listen to me, you repulsive, revolting swine: I demand that you all shut your ever so bothersome holes so that I may speak to you plainly and freely. My name is Doctor Circus, you can call me Mr. Doctor Circus, and this is my play. You will enjoy it with every miserable fiber of your nauseating being or, goddamn you, I will slaughter the lot of you with nary a hint of remorse. And don't think I won't! For, many people have doubted me and they all have fallen at my hand!

Somewhere near the end of his wonderful speech, some rather LOUD WHISPERING has begun by the PERSON FROM THE AUDIENCE. Doctor Circus notices it, stopping dead in his rant and looking out into what should be perceived as the darkness.

DOCTOR CIRCUS: Who is that?

There is no reply.

DOCTOR CIRCUS: *(losing what "cool" he had left)* WHO THE FUCK IS IT?! *(he waits barely a beat before he points to the Person from the Audience)* Was it you? *(he gets no reply)* HEY!!!

Doctor Circus jumps from the stage and walks, quickly, to where the Person from the Audience is sitting [Which will hopefully be in a hard to reach spot.] and puts his face right in front of them.

DOCTOR CIRCUS: Was it you?

PERSON FROM THE AUDIENCE: *(awkwardly)* *Come* on, man.

DOCTOR CIRCUS: "Come on" what?

The Person from the Audience just shrugs.

DOCTOR CIRCUS: Oh, so now you're silent?

There is a long pause as Doctor Circus stares The Person[1] down.

DOCTOR CIRCUS: Come with me.

---

[1] The Person and Person from the Audience are interchangeable. It should be obvious to even a dolt.

Doctor Circus walks away, expecting to be followed. He is, however, not being followed.

DOCTOR CIRCUS: I said, "come with me"!

The Person from the Audience doesn't move. They are far too afraid to do anything, as they should be.

DOCTOR CIRCUS: Oh, aren't you a detestable piece-of-shit?

He walks over to the Person from the Audience and grabs them by the arm. He then proceeds to drag them up, onto the stage. They end up by Doctor Circus's chair CS.

DOCTOR CIRCUS: Now… *(he circles The Person who is very uncomfortable)* What do you have to say?

Doctor Circus then stares down the Person from the Audience and The Person just stares back. There is a stalemate. One demands something to be said, and the other has no idea what they are supposed to say. The Person then realizes that something must be said, lest this silence go on forever.

PERSON FROM THE AUDIENCE: W-w-what do you want me to do?

DOCTOR CIRCUS: You heard me! I asked you what you fucking said that was so important that you felt the need to interrupt the show for these good people. *(he motions to the audience when he says "these good people")*

The Person seemingly had nothing to say. There are things they want to say, but the words do not come Doctor Circus sighs and then, before anyone can comprehend what is happening, he clutches the Person from the Audience's face.

DOCTOR CIRCUS: *(yelling into the Person from the Audience's face)* SO WHAT IS SO IMPORTANT?!

PERSON FROM THE AUDIENCE: *(scared)* I-I-I-

DOCTOR CIRCUS: YOU WHAT?!

PERSON FROM THE AUDIENCE: *(desperate)* I just wanted to know where the bathroom was!

Doctor Circus drops The Person's face and begins to laugh. The Person grabs their face, trying to rub the pain away.

DOCTOR CIRCUS: Oh is that all?

PERSON FROM THE AUDIENCE: Y-yes.

DOCTOR CIRCUS: *(uncharacteristically humble, over-dramatically so)* Well then, may I offer my humblest of apologies. I fear that I've come across as some sort of buffoon. Is there any way that you could ever forgive me?

Doctor Circus looks to The Person. The Person seems wary.

DOCTOR CIRCUS: Could you? *(pause)* Please?

PERSON FROM THE AUDIENCE: *(unsure)* Yes?

DOCTOR CIRCUS: Good. That's good. That does mean, however, that I have a favor that I must ask of you, my new, dear friend. I ask you, my sweet, sweet acquaintance, that you refrain from speaking during the duration of the show once I allow you to rejoin the audience. Do you think you could do that for me?

PERSON FROM THE AUDIENCE: Yes.

DOCTOR CIRCUS: You promise?

PERSON FROM THE AUDIENCE: Yes.

DOCTOR CIRCUS: *(thinking)* Hmmmmm….

Doctor Circus walks around The Person. He sizes them up and looks them over. He judges them harshly with his eyes before he unleashes his verdict.

DOCTOR CIRCUS: Do you want to know something? Hmmm?

PERSON FROM THE AUDIENCE: What?

DOCTOR CIRCUS: I DON'T BELIEVE YOU!

Doctor Circus swings his cane about and takes out The Person's knees from beneath them. They fall back, hitting the back of their head upon the stage. Doctor Circus then begins to beat The Person so realistically that the audience thinks it could, in fact, be happening, and it is, in fact, happening. The Person calls out for help, yet their cries go unheard. No one comes to their aide, and if they do, they are struck down, if not with the cane, then with words. The beating continues. The cane slips from Doctor Circus's hands, whether it's because it breaks, or because it is no longer of use is unsure. He straddles The Person, strangling them as they flail about. After much struggle and strife, The Person goes limp. Doctor Circus then stands and turns back to the audience. He is still trembling with rage.

DOCTOR CIRCUS: IS THERE ANYONE ELSE WITH SOMETHING TO SAY?!

He stands there panting as the audience, as they should, remains silent. [If they jeer, please put them in their place. Precedence should be set here.]

DOCTOR CIRCUS: *(instantly calm)* Good.

Doctor Circus motions OSR and TWO STAGEHANDS come out and pick up The Person's body. Doctor Circus then motions OSL and ANOTHER STAGEHAND comes out, handing Doctor Circus his cane, or, if the original one broke (as it's wont to do- the blasted thing!), a new one is presented to him.

DOCTOR CIRCUS: *(sighing and composing himself, fully)* Now where was I? *(he thinks for a moment)* Ah, yes! My name is Doctor Circus and… *(he motions to the set)* …this is The House of Boxes. *(he laughs for some reason, known only to him)* And this, this is Glee, The Woeful!

At his beckon call, GLEE, THE WOEFUL, enters from SL (woefully) and stands next to Doctor Circus.

DOCTOR CIRCUS: *(once Glee is by him, he motions SR)* And this is Woe, The Gleeful!

Again, at his beckon call, WOE THE GLEEFUL enters from SR and stands on the opposite side of Doctor Circus (the side not held by Glee).

DOCTOR CIRCUS: These two fine fiends are my humble servants and I would like for you to meet them now, before we begin my show. Oh! That reminds me: Before my show begins, I must inform you of a few rules that you must follow in order to enjoy the show to its fullest extent. *(clears his throat)* RULE THE FIRST: You must listen to every word that I have to say. And I mean every elegant, well-crafted syllable. I have toiled over this work for decades. And many decades after that. And, I tell you, humbly, this is a work of pure and unabashed genius. If you miss one syllable of it, you will regret it until your very last dying breath. *(now, again he clears his throat, but in such a way that emphasizes that this throat clearing is more important than the last)* Now, RULE THE SECOND- and this is the most important of all the rules, so please, listen closely. This rule involves one little word. Now this word, this awful, little, repugnant, monosyllabic, cunt of a word, is, without question, the absolute worst word one can say to any one, especially if it is to their face. And, without question, it must never –and I mean NEVER- be uttered within the halls of The House of Boxes. Now I, with my infinite immunity, will utter this word once, and only once. ONCE! But it will only be said so that none of you make the same mistake that one man did once, long ago. Oh, so long ago. *(he takes a moment to reminisce about the time in his life from which he is pulling this memory)* Ha! So yes, that word, that fucking word, that word that you must never utter in these halls so hallowed is: *(he shivers before he says it)* …love… *(he gags as though he is about it vomit. [It should be noted, here, that if anyone does, in fact, gain such hubris as to say "love", they should be excused from the theatre posthaste in a manner that belittles them so. An example should be made of such swine.])* Yes, that word makes me wretch with such disdain. It ravishes me right to my bones. So it must never be uttered- uttered- UTTERED! And if it is, may god have mercy on your soul. For, even if you utter it under your breath here tonight, trust me, I will hear it and I will know. If that is the case, I will make sure that you get what is coming to you. It could be whilst you're driving home in your oh-so-fashionable automobile and then you'll hear a rap-a-tap-tap from the boot of your horseless carriage and you'll pull over. You'll feel the need to inspect the noise. I know you will, you know who you are. You'll want to inspect what could be causing such a questionable racket. Once you open the boot, however, no matter how full of hubris you may feel now, you will defecate all over yourself, for in the boot you will find a certain Mastermind of Malice hiding in there, with a blade resembling this: *(he then produces a dagger from somewhere within his jacket and holds it to the audience so that the blade glistens in the light)* And I promise you, my dear fellow or madam, that he will force it into you over and over and over and over and OVER AGAIN! He'll thrust it in until the breath that you breathed while uttering that vile word is no more. That word whose meaning will escape you when you look that madman in the eyes and blink your last blunk. *(he ponders this for a second)* Or, you know, better yet, this mega-minded mortal might wait until you've arrived home. He would want you to be safe in your little pre-made palace. A home built by hands you paid for. Then he will make his presence known. Yes! Perhaps this person, who is not me, will bide his time under your bed, or in that closet you rarely use, the one you use for umbrellas or guest's coats. He will breath, softly and calmly. He will wait. And wait. And wait. Maybe even for days. Until one day, your dog or your cat or your child or your postman will go missing and you'll ponder its whereabouts, attempting each night to wrap your mind around such things. Maybe you'll lay awake at night thinking about it, maybe you'll be overcome with guilt, or maybe, still, you'll forget about this night and sleep soundly. Maybe you'll think it is just a circumstance of life. Maybe the disappearance has nothing to do with you? But then one day, oh one day, no matter how you feel about it —and this I promise you- you will discover that there is a smell in your home. It will be a smell so pungent that it will haunt your home. Your breakfast, your lunch, your dinner, they will all be tainted by this inescapable scent. You'll try your damndest to track it down. It will be an all-consuming quest. You will search and hunt and pursue and inquire until it tires you so. But then you will find that what you seek. You'll be lead to under your bed –a place you'd checked a thousand times- or that closet you rarely use –another place you'd scoured previously- and there you'll find Rex or Isis or Cassandra or Ian or Mr. Postman. And, oh, what is this? It appears as though someone has fed upon them slightly? This once-precious dead thing. It seems as though someone needed sustenance and they turned to your little darling for the need that must be met. When you realize this, you'll shriek in horror –it will be something instinctual you do- and you'll back away from the disgusting muddle your eyes just gazed upon. You'll turn away from it –it is an "it" now- and you'll search for answers. You will find none. You will then most likely involve the police. They will come, as they're wont to do, and they will search your home. They will look for clues and such. They will find none. But the fact that they "are on it" will give you some comfort. You'll be able to lie in your bed again. It won't be the same bed. It will most likely be in a different room. It might even be a different place. But, still, you will find a place to lay your head and you will lay it there. You won't feel quite safe enough, though, to fall asleep. You will feel that slumber is persistent, however. You will try to fight it. How could you sleep under such turmoil? Even with that pulling on your mind, sleep will still pull its wool over your eyes. You will convince yourself that a goodnight's rest is best. And now, then –then as you're about to close your eyes- that's when there will be a shadow that will cause your eyes to shoot open abruptly, but you'll be too caught up in half-sleep to process anything completely. You will then feel a pressure in your bed, as though someone is joining you –or you and your partner (if your pathetic pathos-ridden person could trick someone into partnering with you). Regardless, this will cause you to shoot up and as you do, you will be met with a sharp pain in your gut and a familiar face smirking at you, becoming the last thing you will ever see. *(he laughs at the thought of this, it brings him great joy)* Oh, my word, those memories, how they tug on the strings of my heart. *(he remembers that he's in the middle of something)* Where was I? Oh, yes! RULE THE THIRD: *(pause)*

Doctor Circus thinks about what the third rule could be, yet, for some reason, it escapes him. He looks to Glee.

DOCTOR CIRCUS: *(to Glee)* Do you remember what the third rule is?

Glee, The Woeful shakes her head. Doctor Circus sighs and disappointedly turns to Woe, The Gleeful.

DOCTOR CIRCUS: *(to Woe)* Do you?

Woe, The Gleeful shakes his head. This causes Doctor Circus to sigh in a mixture of disappointment and frustration.

DOCTOR CIRCUS: *(composes himself after this disappointment)* Well then... Never mind! We should probably start the show. THE LIGHTS! *(he stomps his cane down and the house lights are cut abruptly)* THE CURTAINS! *(again, he stomps his cane and the curtains begin to close)*

As the curtains close Glee, The Woeful and Woe, The Gleeful exit behind the closing curtain.

DOCTOR CIRCUS: *(with all the pomp and circumstance in the world)* Now, ladies and gentlemen, please abide by the rules and enjoy the show! *(as he exits the stage)* SET THE GODDAMN STAGE!

He exits fully, laughing maniacally all the while. The curtains close in full once he passes through them.

END RANT I.

ACT I

STAGEHANDS bring out the TREE PROPS and the CAR FRONT and place them LSR as THE ACTOR PLAYING "JOHN" [read as JOHN] and THE ACTRESS PLAYING "JANE" 1 [read as JANE 1] enter and crouch by the hood of the car. Jane 1 goes limp in John's arms and John holds her, shaking her slightly in a frantic, yet gentile fashion as the car BEGINS TO SMOKE.

JOHN: *(worried)* Jane? Jane?! Oh my god, Jane, please wake up.

Jane 1 stirs and looks up at John as though she is coming out of a daze.

JANE 1: *(slightly bewildered)* John? Is that really you? Oh my. I just had the most horrendous dream. What happened?

JOHN: We were in an accident, my dear. A deer ran out in front of us and I swerved and hit that tree.

John motions to the car hood, which happens to not have a tree on it. This faux pas doesn't go unnoticed and John looks around like he doesn't know how to continue. He is a dumb actor, after all.

DOCTOR CIRCUS: *(OS)* Damn it all, go! Go!

A STAGEHAND comes out and puts a TREE BRANCH on the car's smoking hood. He then hurries off, trying to not be noticed in a very noticeable way.

JOHN: *(as though he is giving a poor improv)* Yes… Um… I ran into that tree there trying to miss that poor animal.

JANE 1: Oh no, did you hit it?

JOHN: …Yes…

They begin to stand and look at the car.

JANE 1: Poor deer.

JOHN: Oh, I'm fine.

JANE 1: I meant the deer, dear, not you, dear.

They hold for a laugh that hopefully will not come.

DOCTOR CIRCUS: *(OS/harsh whisper)* Be better.

JOHN: *(trying to make up for the failure)* Well I don't think the car will be able to run, I think I'm going to try to walk to that gas station we passed awhile back. You stay here with the car, for no particular reason.

JANE 1: What? Why should I stay here next to these woods all by myself?

JOHN: I don't know. Aren't you hurt or something?

JANE 1: No, so I'm going with you.

JOHN: Okay, fine, I guess that makes sense. But hey, you know what we should do?

JANE 1: What?

JOHN: We should take the scenic route through these woods here. I think it might be romantic.

JANE 1: Wait, aren't these woods haunted?

A 'bum-bum-bum' comes from OS.

JOHN: Oh, you know me, I don't believe in that kind of mumbo-jumbo.

JANE 1: Well then, we should be fine!

JOHN: Yes, we should! Shall we go now?

JANE 1: Yes, we should.

JOHN: Well then away we go.

They take each other's hands lovingly as they walk across the stage. All of a sudden, a strange HUMMING comes from OSL.

JANE 1: What is that?

JOHN: What? I don't hear anything.

JANE 1: You don't hear that?

The two of them stop and stand perfectly still trying to pinpoint where the eerie humming is coming from.

JOHN: Oh yeah, I do. What is that?

JANE 1: I don't know. *(looks OSL, the direction of the hum, and sees something horrifying)* Oh my god. What are they?

JOHN: Who? *(he follows her gaze OSL and a look of curious horror grows across his face, it is delightful)* I... I don't know.

JANE 1: I don't like this, John.

JOHN: Me either.

DOCTOR CIRCUS: (OS) Neither!

JOHN: *(correcting)* Me neither.

It is then that Glee, the Woeful, and Woe, the Gleeful enter from behind the car LSL in a manner that can only be described as whimsical. Although, they do look creepy, delightfully so. They continue to hum off-key as they enter, which abruptly ends when they notice John and Jane 1 standing across the stage from them. They snigger in a way which appears to make the couple uncomfortable.

GLEE, THE WOEFUL: Now, brother, who is it over there that I see?

WOE, THE GLEEFUL: Oh, sister, I do not know why you bother asking me.

Glee frowns and Woe smiles at the couple across the stage from them, as they try to size John and Jane 1 up.

WOE, THE GLEEFUL: It appears as though they are lost in travel.

GLEE, THE WOEFUL: Are they aware of their fate which shall unravel?

WOE, THE GLEEFUL: I doubt it, dear sister, how could they know?

GLEE, THE WOEFUL: A good point, my brother. To them we must go.

They laugh, playfully, to one another as they creep overcautiously, considering they've been seen already, to John and Jane 1 who seem very, very uncomfortable.

GLEE, THE WOEFUL: Hello, fine strangers. How do you do?

WOE, THE GLEEFUL: I am Woe; this is Glee, 'tis nice to meet you.

John and Jane 1 appear to be frozen in fear as they stare at the two jesters. John then decides to shake it off and attempts to talk to them.

JOHN: Um... Hi... I'm John. *(he extends his hand and Glee and Woe just stare at it. He awkwardly brings his hand back to himself, trying to play it off.)* And this is my wife, Jane. Um... We seem to be having a little bit of car problems. Do you think you could give us some assistance?

WOE, THE GLEEFUL: Why sure, my good man, whatever you need.

GLEE, THE WOEFUL: We'll do what we can, no matter the deed.

JOHN: Well... Do you have a car of some sort? Or maybe a phone we could use to call a tow truck or something?

GLEE, THE WOEFUL: Unfortunately, in those ways, we cannot assist.

WOE, THE GLEEFUL: Yet there is one option in which you can enlist.

JOHN: What option is that?

WOE, THE GLEEFUL: Follow us to the mansion on high.

GLEE, THE WOEFUL: And there you can meet one special guy.

WOE, THE GLEEFUL: He will help you with everything at his hand.

GLEE, THE WOEFUL: He is perfectly respectable, the gentlest man.

JOHN: Does he have a phone?

GLEE, THE WOEFUL: I assure you this man has any desire.

WOE, THE GLEEFUL: And if he does not you may call her a liar.

JOHN: Well... *(turning to Jane 1)* What do you think?

JANE 1: *(whisper)* I don't like this, John.

JOHN: *(whisper)* Well, what should we do?

JANE 1: *(whisper)* Let's just go to the gas station.

JOHN: *(whisper)* But what if this place is closer?

JANE 1: *(whisper)* I don't know. I don't like how they-

JOHN: *(to Glee and Woe)* Is this mansion far?

JANE 1: *(protesting)* Jonathan!

JOHN: What, Jane?

JANE 1: *(whisper)* I really, really don't like this.

JOHN: It'll be okay, honey.

WOE, THE GLEEFUL: Yes, my sweet, I assure you all is fine.

GLEE, THE WOEFUL: Yes, our friend, he will be so kind.

JOHN: See, honey?

She looks at John and then over to Glee and Woe, then back to John.

JANE 1: Alright, we can go I guess.

Glee and Woe laugh, a little too maniacally for Jane 1's comfort. John doesn't seem to notice.

WOE, THE GLEEFUL: Oh joy, the master will surely be pleased.

GLEE, THE WOEFUL: Yes, a little company is all that he needs.

JOHN: Wait, who is "the master"?

GLEE & WOE: All in good time.

They smile wickedly as they lead the couple over to LCS. When they arrive to the direct center of the curtains, the curtains open to reveal THE HOUSE OF BOXES EXTERIOR: a shoddy forest and in the middle of it all, A CARDBOARD CUTOUT OF A

LAVISH MANSION that appears to be made from hundreds (if not thousands) of colorful boxes.

JOHN: Is that the mansion?

GLEE & WOE: Yes.

They begin to walk towards the mansion. Jane 1 walks slowly, which causes John to walk slowly as well. Distance grows between them and the jesters.

JANE 1: *(whisper)* John, I do not like this one bit.

JOHN: *(whisper)* I know, honey, but we'll just go in and use their phone and be on our way, really quick.

JANE 1: *(whispering)* But it's late. What if they can't help us until morning? I don't want to stay the night there.

Glee and Woe stop abruptly and turn to face John and Jane 1 who look as though they've just been caught doing something they shouldn't be doing.

GLEE, THE WOEFUL: Mouths that whisper should stay shut.

WOE, THE GLEEFUL: And throats that murmur deserve to be cut.

They continue to stare at the couple who look rather frightened.

JOHN: Oh, we're sorry, we weren't saying anythi-

GLEE & WOE: *(interrupting)* Please, follow us.

They gesture towards the house and let the couple pass through them and towards the house cutout. When they get to the cardboard house it's as tall as they are. John and Jane 1 stand there, not knowing what to do. Glee and Woe walk up, look at them, and then walk behind the house.

GLEE & WOE: Follow us.

Glee and Woe cross behind the house and exit USL. John and Jane 1 look at one another and then follow.

As they exit STAGEHANDS rush on in a wave to redress the set so that it now becomes THE HOUSE OF BOXES INTERIOR, complete with a MANTEL and PORTRAIT. At the end of the quick redress Doctor Circus reenters the stage and goes to sit on a CHAIR that has been placed SL. Just as he takes his seat, Glee, Woe and the couple enter from SR in a quick manner and stand at attention.

GLEE, THE WOEFUL: It is with all the pleasure that the world can muster...

WOE, THE GLEEFUL: ...That we introduce to you...

GLEE, THE WOEFUL: ...The Mastermind of Malice...

WOE, THE GLEEFUL: ...The Esquire of Evil...

GLEE, THE WOEFUL: ...The Knight of Naughty...

WOE, THE GLEEFUL: ...The Warrior of the Wicked...

GLEE, THE WOEFUL: ...The Vicar of Vices...

WOE, THE GLEEFUL: ...The Crowned King of Corruption...

GLEE, THE WOEFUL: ...The Duke of Disaster...

WOE, THE GLEEFUL: ...The One...

GLEE, THE WOEFUL: ...The Only...

Doctor Circus stands excitedly.

DOCTOR CIRCUS: Me!

He holds for applause, none is given, so he stomps his cane on the floor which prompts the jesters to applaud which, in turn, causes the couple to applaud. Yet, John and Jane 1 look confused. Doctor Circus notices and looks at them with his head cocked, inquisitively.

DOCTOR CIRCUS: *(to Jane 1 and John)* Well what on earth can I do for you, my newest and dearest friends?

JOHN: Well, um...

John looks over at Jane 1, not knowing what he should say to Doctor Circus.

DOCTOR CIRCUS: Go on...

JOHN: It's just that, I... Um... We... They...

DOCTOR CIRCUS: *(losing it)* Out with it!

JOHN: Sorry, sir, I mean- well wait, I don't believe we've gotten your name.

DOCTOR CIRCUS: *(mockingly sarcastic)* Oh, I'm sorry.

Was that introduction that my oldest and loyalist accomplices gave to you not a good one? Did you not understand it?

JOHN: *(hesitantly)* Well, no. It's just that they didn't-

DOCTOR CIRCUS: You need to speak faster!

JOHN: *(quicker)* Well, no. It's just we didn't get your name.

DOCTOR CIRCUS: I'm sorry, I don't understand you. Are you speaking with an accent?

JOHN: *(unsure of how to respond)* N-no?

DOCTOR CIRCUS: What? *(looking to Glee and Woe)* I don't understand him. Do you two? *(he doesn't wait for them to answer; instead he turns to Jane 1)* Do you?

JANE 1: Y-y-yes.

DOCTOR CIRCUS: Well then what the fuck is he on about?

JANE 1: He's trying to say that they *(motions to Glee and Woe with a hint of disgust)* never said your name.

DOCTOR CIRCUS: Who never said my name?

JANE 1: *(again, motions to Glee and Woe)* Them.

Doctor Circus turns to look where she is motioning and seems as though he is startled by Glee and Woe. He leans over to Jane 1 who flinches as he comes near.

DOCTOR CIRCUS: *(whispering)* You can see them too?

JANE 1: *(not knowing what to say)* Yes...?

DOCTOR CIRCUS: Oh good. That solves a lot of problems I was having when I wrote this. *(he laughs to himself)* Well then, I suppose true formalities are in order, no?

He walks back over to the chair he was sitting in and sits down as though none of this had ever happened before. He then coughs and looks over to Glee and Woe who get the picture and escort the couple back out of the room. Three beats pass and then Doctor Circus stomps his cane down. Glee, Woe, John and Jane 1 reenter in the same manner that they did before, all of them stand at attention. Woe mimics the sound of an announcement horn.

GLEE, THE WOEFUL: Even though you both are worthless!

WOE, THE GLEEFUL: We present to you: Doctor Circus!

Doctor Circus stands, expecting applause, yet again, he gets none. He does not like this one bit.

DOCTOR CIRCUS: *(outburst)* DAMN YOU ALL!!!

Glee, Woe, John and Jane 1 are all taken aback

WOE, THE GLEEFUL: What is it, sir?

GLEE, THE WOEFUL: Yes, how can-

DOCTOR CIRCUS: What does it say in the script?!

WOE, THE GLEEFUL: *(breaking character)* What?

DOCTOR CIRCUS: *(through gritted teeth)* What does it say in the goddamn script?!

WOE, THE GLEEFUL: *(looking to Glee)* I-I don't know what you're talking about sir, I-

DOCTOR CIRCUS: Did you even read the fucking thing?!

Doctor Circus throws his hands up in an exacerbated fashion and looks at each and everyone on stage. They are all scared silent. He rubs his eyes before he walks over to Woe, the Gleeful.

DOCTOR CIRCUS: Damnit, Woe! *(he turns to Glee, she cowers)* Did you read it?! *(he turns to Jane 1 and John)* Did you?

None of them give any sort of answer.

DOCTOR CIRCUS: Well damn it all! Are you not aware of what a script is for? It's for these kinds of instances! It says, in the wonderful script that I wonderfully wrote and you apparently never bothered to read, that after I am introduced I stand and you four are to applaud me with smiles of adoration adorning your faces, FOR I AM YOUR SAVIOR! *(everyone still looks at him as though they are very confused)* So I suppose what we shall do is start again! From the top!

JOHN: The whole top?

GLEE, THE WOEFUL: Like from the car?

DOCTOR CIRCUS: *(nearly losing it)* No! No! No! No! No! Why does no one understand me? *(dropping to his knees as though he has been defeated)* Why was I cursed with this horrid cast? *(to the heavens)* Why?!

Doctor Circus then exercises his god-given right to behave as he wishes and he begins to shriek and wail as he rolls across the stage, taking breaks to crawl around and beat the stage itself with his fists. He makes strange noises and curses and rolls and pouts. He does this to show to his supposed cast mates just how he feels. Then, as quickly as all of it started, he stops. Doctor Circus rises and dusts off his tailcoat.

DOCTOR CIRCUS: *(a deep, centering breath)* We will be taking it from the top of this scene. You will go off stage, you will come back on stage, I will be introduced and you will applaud, or so may you be damned!

No one moves.

DOCTOR CIRCUS: NOW!

As though that one word was a threat on all of their lives, Glee, Woe, John and Jane 1 scamper OSL. Doctor Circus doesn't even bother to sit down this time. He just impatiently taps his foot as they exit. As soon as they're off, he stomps his cane and they come back out quickly, standing at attention.

GLEE, THE WOEFUL: *(rushed)* May we present to you with no disdain...

WOE, THE GLEEFUL: *(rushed, also)* Doctor Circus, for that is his name!

They applaud uproariously, like they were supposed to, as Doctor Circus outstretches his arms and bathes in the glory they are bestowing upon him. He takes several bows and waves his hands, smiling all the while. It goes on for quite some time, but Doctor Circus is able to keep the same vim and vigor throughout the ovation.

DOCTOR CIRCUS: Why, thank you. Thank you. All this fuss truly is unnecessary. *(he approaches the group)* And who are you two?

John and Jane 1 look at one another and then back to Doctor Circus.

JOHN: Oh, um, I'm John. John Doe. *(he puts his arm around Jane 1)* and this is my wife, Jane.

DOCTOR CIRCUS: John and Jane Doe, eh?

JOHN: Yes sir.

DOCTOR CIRCUS: Oh how wonderfully trite and predictably cliché. *(to the audience/angrily)* Don't you dare judge me, you peons of naught! *(back to John and Jane 1)* Pardon me, where are my manners? May I ask, why have you entered my gracious and supreme abode, my unmatched palace?

JOHN: Well sir, we-

DOCTOR CIRCUS: *(angry)* Was I talking to you, boy?!

Everyone looks at him as though they are a deer in headlights.

JOHN: *(unsure but positive)* Yes?

DOCTOR CIRCUS: Oh, well sorry, then. Please continue.

JOHN: Well, um, is there any way that we could possibly use your phone?

DOCTOR CIRCUS: Excuse me?

JOHN: We would like to use your phone... *(remembering to be polite)* Um... sir.

DOCTOR CIRCUS: I am terribly sorry, but I cannot understand your dialect. Where are you from?

JOHN: *(as though it is made up)* Uh... Massachusetts[2]?

DOCTOR CIRCUS: *(turning to Jane 1)* I'm sorry but what is he saying?

JANE 1: He's saying that we are from Massachusetts[3] and that we would like to use your phone.

DOCTOR CIRCUS: Oh my, well aren't we a long way from home?

JOHN: Yes we are, and we're-

DOCTOR CIRCUS: *(angry)* Was I talking to you?!

JOHN: No...

---

[2] In non-American versions, this is different. For example, in England and Ireland it is "Cork", in Europe it is "Oslo", in Mexico it is "Vera Cruz", in The Far East it is "Gunma", in the Middle East it is "Karachi", in Australia it is "Alice Springs", in Africa it is "Cleveland", etc.

[3] see Footnote 2.

DOCTOR CIRCUS: HA! I got you! Thought you could slip by me, eh? No one slips by Doctor Circus with this sort of tomfoolery!

JOHN: I'm sorry.

DOCTOR CIRCUS: It's fine, you're stupidity is comeuppance enough. *(turns back to Jane 1)* So I believe you were saying something about needing to use my bone?

JANE 1: *(incredibly uncomfortable)* Oh lord, no!

DOCTOR CIRCUS: So you were not attempting to lay with me?

JANE 1: *(without hesitation for some reason)* No. Never.

DOCTOR CIRCUS: *(angry)* Then why would you bring up wanting my bone? There's a special place in Hell for harlots[4] like you!

JANE 1: *(trying to back track)* No, no, no, I wasn't saying "bone", I was saying "phone". With a "pha-".

DOCTOR CIRCUS: Oh. *(trying to laugh if off)* Well, I suppose this makes more sense. But how dare you tempt me so. *(he bites at her sexually)*

JANE 1: I wasn't trying to tempt you, I-

---

[4] It should be noted that Doctor Circus has the upmost respect for women. Jane 1 (and Jane 2, for that matter), doesn't deserve that respect, however, so that is why this term is alright to use here.

DOCTOR CIRCUS: Oh, you weren't were you? *(coyly)* I'm sure.

JANE 1: Absolutely not.

DOCTOR CIRCUS: *(sheepishly)* Well you'll come around, they all do. *(he turns to Glee and Woe)* Now take them to their rooms! We should all get some rest before the night comes!

Doctor Circus begins to stride OS, but no one else moves. They stare at Doctor Circus and he notices this so he stops. He seems very confused by what is happening.

DOCTOR CIRCUS: *(looking to the cast)* What? *(looks OS)* Oh. *(back to the cast)* Are we not there yet?

WOE, THE GLEEFUL: Um… No…

DOCTOR CIRCUS: Oh, well, silly me, I guess you did read the script though, eh? *(laughs, then thinks)* So where exactly are we?

JOHN: The phone.

DOCTOR CIRCUS: *(to Jane 1)* Eh?

JANE 1: The phone.

DOCTOR CIRCUS: *(fed up)* Madam, for the last time! I will not take you to bed!

JANE 1: No, we already did that part. We're at the actual phone part.

DOCTOR CIRCUS: Oh, well then. Sorry. *(he "gets back into character")* Can we take it from your line, Jane?

JANE 1: Yes.

DOCTOR CIRCUS: Okay. Go.

JANE 1: We need-

DOCTOR CIRCUS: Wait! *(he sighs and shakes off the bad take they just did)* Okay, go now.

JANE 1: We need to use your phone.

DOCTOR CIRCUS: Oh well, that is indeed quite a problem.

JOHN: What do you mean?

John's speaking out of turn is like nails on a chalkboard to Doctor Circus and he is overwhelmed with immense frustration. It's so much more frustrating than anything on this abysmal planet. He looks at John but is unable to even speak to John. He just shakes a little, gripping his cane.

JANE 1: *(stepping in to save John)* What do you mean?

DOCTOR CIRCUS: *(shaking off his hatred for John[5])* I mean, that we do not have a phone in this dwelling. Phones are a disastrous affront to privacy!

---

[5] This is impossible, but he is a trained actor and is good at least pretending that it is possible, despite how infuriatingly stupid John is and will always be.

Just then, as if a man OS is making it happen, a telephone begins to ring. They all stop and look SL, the direction the sound is coming from.

JOHN: Then what is that?

JANE 1: That sounded an awful lot like a telephone.

DOCTOR CIRCUS: Well that shows what you know about stagecraft. That's merely a soundman with a sound box, standing offstage, pushing that button that make the sound, which is placed there for the most comedic of timings.

JOHN: A sound man?

DOCTOR CIRCUS: Yes, you dolt. Do you not listen? Can you not see?

Doctor Circus points with his cane OSL, towards the assumed soundman that may or may not be there. Everyone looks, but no one says anything.

DOCTOR CIRCUS: *(fed up with all of their stupidity)* Ugh! Fine!

Doctor Circus strides OSL as he pulls out his dagger. We hear the sound of a horrific death[6] followed by a very loud thud. Doctor Circus then strides back on stage with a SOUND BOX in his hand. He wipes blood off his brow and throws the box onto the floor in front of everyone.

---

[6] The sound of his murder resounded throughout the auditorium. It was like the yelps of a hyena as it is mauled by a lion, except within each yelp the words "no" or "stop" could clearly be heard.

DOCTOR CIRCUS: I regret to inform you, my friends, that our phone is dead.

JOHN: It's dead? How can it be dead?

DOCTOR CIRCUS: Can you not hear the storm?

The couple listens, there is no sound.

JOHN and JANE 1: No.

DOCTOR CIRCUS: Damn it! *(he pounds his cane on the floor and looks around as though something is supposed to happen)* Damn that soundman!

GLEE, THE WOEFUL: *(whispering)* Sir.

DOCTOR CIRCUS: *(fed up)* What!?

Glee and Woe look at each other. Woe leans in and whispers to Doctor Circus. Doctor Circus nods his head as he listens to what apparently seems like bad news. This news seems to get to him, but the show must go on. He shakes it off and gets back into the performance.

DOCTOR CIRCUS: *(commanding)* Well then you two go and do it!

Glee and Woe rush OS. There is a lot of rustling and commotion coming from off.

DOCTOR CIRCUS: *(calling off)* Are you ready?

GLEE and WOE: *(OS)* Yes!

DOCTOR CIRCUS: Good *(he turns to face the couple)* Can you hear the rain?

The couple listens and again, nothing happens. Doctor Circus brings his cane down and the SOUND OF THUNDER BOOMS[7] in from all around, while the lights flicker on and off to give the illusion of lightening.

JOHN: Oh no!

JANE 1: What are we going to do?

DOCTOR CIRCUS: Why you should stay here, of course. If you go out there you might get struck by lightening. Or maybe catch a cold. Or just get wet. All of which seem a rather uncomfortable predicament to place yourselves into.

JOHN: *(sharing an unsure glance with Jane 1)* No, I don't really think we could.

DOCTOR CIRCUS: Oh, nonsense, you can stay here until morning and then we can take you to one of those fancy fueling stations that seem to be all the rage nowadays.

JANE 1: I really don't think we can do that.

JOHN: Yeah, I really don't think it's raining that bad.

Doctor Circus bangs his cane on the stage floor and thunder and lightening ensue.

---

[7] If one is unable to conjure thunder this way themselves a thunder board may be used.

DOCTOR CIRCUS: Are you positive? That sounds just awful. *(rather wickedly)* I insist you stay.

Jane 1 nudges John to chime in.

JOHN: Oh, um, I don't think-

DOCTOR CIRCUS: *(commanding)* Stay!

JOHN: *(frightened)* Stay!

Jane 1 nudges John disapprovingly. John shrugs at her with the shoulders of a milquetoast.

DOCTOR CIRCUS: Oh wonderful! *(calling off)* Glee! Woe!

Glee and Woe rush onstage.

GLEE, THE WOEFUL: Yes sir, what is it you need done?

WOE, THE GLEEFUL: Is it a deed of business or a deed of fun?

DOCTOR CIRCUS: Oh, one of fun, of course. I believe that we need to show these two to their sleeping quarters and then prepare a dinner- neigh, a feast! –for these fine guests of ours. Surely they must be famished, for I wrote so in the script!

WOE, THE GLEEFUL: Yes, of course, we'll do what we can.

GLEE, THE WOEFUL: But shouldn't the tour be led by your hand?

Doctor Circus thinks about this for a moment. He looks around as though he doesn't know what to do, but then it comes back to him.

DOCTOR CIRCUS: Yes, of course, please prepare the stage for dinner time. We'll be there upon the cessation of the tour. *(to John and Jane 1)* Please gather your things and follow me to your quarters!

Doctor Circus strides off SL as though he were a marching band conductor. He uses his cane like a baton. Jane 1 and John look at one another, and then to Glee and Woe, who motion for them to follow Doctor Circus. They do. Upon their exit, Woe and Glee motion off SR for the STAGEHANDS to come out and move everything about, setting up the stage so that it looks like a DINING ROOM. When it is all done, Woe and Glee stand there, with trays of food in their hands at the head of the table. This happens just in time for Doctor Circus to enter SR, followed by Jane 1 and John, who seem very, very uncomfortable.

DOCTOR CIRCUS: *(in the middle of his tour)* ...and that room back there, the one we just passed, is The Sodomy Chamber. Now that shouldn't be confused with The Chamber of Rape; sodomy should never, ever be forced. But yeah, interesting fact about The Sodomy Chamber: its walls are made of lead. It's so God's prying eyes can't peek in. It's more for his benefit, than ours. Curiosity killed the cat after all, and what would we do if God went and killed himself? *(answering his own question)* Live freely and happily, I suppose. *(he laughs, but no one else does and this obviously affects him)* Well anyway, this is the lovely dying room.

JOHN: Did you say "dying" room?

DOCTOR CIRCUS: Why no, this is the dining room

you daft fool, this is where we dine! Although, I suppose it could have two meanings. Oh! *(motioning SL)* Off that way is the courtyard and bathing hall, unfortunately we are out of water, however. And down that way *(motioning LSL)*, are the wings of the stage. That's where the stagehands stay, and most of the set that is not being used. Do you see? There's the mantle from before. There's also more to see back that way. *(motioning SR, as he does this he notices the curtains)* Oh! And these! These are the curtains! Aren't they just magnificent? Yes. *(he looks up at them as though he is very proud, before he looks out, into the audience, and his demeanor shifts to disappointment)* Oh, and that's the audience. Pay no mind to them, they have no idea what they're doing with their pathetic lives. Can you believe they actually paid to be here?

Doctor Circus laughs at this and turns back to face the group, focusing mainly on his jesters.

DOCTOR CIRCUS: Is the food ready?

GLEE, THE WOEFUL: Yes sir, I hope you'll find it as you've wished.

WOE, THE GLEEFUL: We've fit your specifications on every single dish.

DOCTOR CIRCUS: That sounds very good. *(to John and Jane 1)* Join me, if you will.

Doctor Circus motions to the table for them to sit. They all sit as Glee and Woe serve them.

DOCTOR CIRCUS: My! This looks delicious! *(to the couple)* Does it not?

JOHN: It looks very good.

JANE 1: Yes, what is it?

DOCTOR CIRCUS: I'm not quite sure. What is this, Glee?

Glee whispers into Doctor Circus's ear.

DOCTOR CIRCUS: *(delighted)* Oh really?

Glee nods.

DOCTOR CIRCUS: Well that is very interesting.

John and Jane 1 look over to Doctor Circus as though he is about to tell them. He doesn't though, instead he just begins to dig in to the meal as though he hasn't eaten in quite some time. John and Jane 1 look at one another.

JOHN: Well?

DOCTOR CIRCUS: Well what?

JANE 1: What are we eating?

DOCTOR CIRCUS: You wouldn't believe me if I told you.

JOHN: Well, try us.

DOCTOR CIRCUS: Try you?

JOHN: Yes.

DOCTOR CIRCUS: *(offended)* Sir! I have not eaten

the flesh of a man in years! How dare you tempt me! Do you know how hard it is to stave such cravings?!

JOHN: No, I wasn't-

DOCTOR CIRCUS: *(less offended)* I suppose I can't judge you, really, though. I guess it is quite understandable. Human flesh is quite delectable, you know this of course.

JANE 1: Will you please just tell us what we're currently eating, please?

DOCTOR CIRCUS: Oh yes of course, it's a Bunyip. *(looking to Glee)* Am I saying that right? "Bun-Yip"?

Glee nods.

JOHN: And what is a Bunyip?

DOCTOR CIRCUS: It's kind of a seal, but in a more wicked, less attractive kind of way. It positively scares the life out of the Aborigines.

JOHN and JANE 1: Oh…

There's an uncomfortable silence that lasts for a very long amount of time.

JOHN: So how long have you lived here?

DOCTOR CIRCUS: Oh, as long as I can remember.

JANE 1: Well how long is that?

Doctor Circus looks up at her with a bit of malice in his eyes[8].

DOCTOR CIRCUS: *(matter-of-factly)* Long enough.

JANE 1: Oh.

JOHN: Well it's a very fine place you have here, Doctor Circus.

DOCTOR CIRCUS: *(correcting)* Mister Doctor Circus. And thank you.

JANE 1: That's a very interesting name…

DOCTOR CIRCUS: Thank you.

Doctor Circus digs back into his food. Jane 1 and John look around uncomfortably, at Doctor Circus, at each other, and then at Glee and Woe who are looking off, standing at attention. Doctor Circus looks at them looking at Glee and Woe. He then turns to Glee and Woe.

DOCTOR CIRCUS: *(Glee and Woe)* You can leave us now.

Glee and Woe bow down and exit SR. Doctor Circus watches them do this and then he turns to the couple.

DOCTOR CIRCUS: So… *(he thinks of what could be appropriate dinnertime conversation)* How do you feel about death?

JOHN: Excuse me?

---

[8] It is extremely rude to ask someone's age, especially when you're a guest in their home.

DOCTOR CIRCUS: Death: how do you feel about it- John, was it?

JOHN: Um… It's bad I guess?

DOCTOR CIRCUS: You guess? *(he scoffs and looks at Jane 1)* And what about you, lady? What to you think about it?

JANE 1: About death? I think it's a bad thing.

DOCTOR CIRCUS: Well it seems that both of you have the same opinion. So I ask you now: Why do you think it is such a bad thing?

JANE 1: Well how is it not a bad thing?

DOCTOR CIRCUS: Some believe that death is freeing. Some believe that it is life that is the "bad thing". I guess I'm just curious why you're on the side of the fence that you are on.

JANE 1: Is that what you think?

DOCTOR CIRCUS: I don't really think that was what I asked. I believe I inquired on your beliefs, not mine.

JOHN: *(butting in)* Well, I don't know, I guess that I, at least, view death as something to be afraid of.

DOCTOR CIRCUS: So would you say you're afraid of death?

JOHN: Yes, I would say that I am.

DOCTOR CIRCUS: *(smirking devilishly)* Well that is just delightful to know. *(turning to Jane 1)* And do you share the same fear of death as your husband here?

JANE 1: Yes, I do. I just think it's just- It's just the 'unknowness' of it all.

DOCTOR CIRCUS: So you fear the unknown?

JANE 1: Sometimes, yes.

DOCTOR CIRCUS: Do you fear me?

There is an uncomfortable silence as Doctor Circus looks at her as though he is looking into her very soul.

JANE 1: *(obviously lying)* No.

DOCTOR CIRCUS: Good! *(to John)* And what do you think of me?

JOHN: You seem to be as nice as the next guy.

DOCTOR CIRCUS: Well I suppose that is a good thing, no?

JOHN: Yes, it is.

DOCTOR CIRCUS: Well good then. I don't know. I've always found death to be a touchy subject, which is why I use it as an ice breaker. I've always found it to be so intriguing, what you can discern from somebody based on how they feel about it. Most people, like yourselves, tend to have an opposing view on the subject from my own. I think that death is a wonderful thing. A beautiful thing. How can the state that you'll spend the majority of your existence in be a truly bad thing? I mean we'll all be dead longer than we've ever lived, right? To me, that would make it seem as though that is our natural state. We were born to die. We shouldn't fear it. Don't get me wrong, however, I can understand why it can be perceived as frightening.

JOHN: I guess there really is no reason for it to be frightening though. Now that I'm thinking about it.

DOCTOR CIRCUS: Well, I don't know, it's like my old priest, Father Noonan used to say: *(he stands abruptly and begins to act as though someone has thrown him onto the table and he is being held there with much force)* "NO DOCTOR CIRCUS! NO! HOW COULD YOU DO THIS?! WHY?! *(continuing on, miming out a scene that no one else sees)* "IS THAT A CHAINSAW?! DOCTOR CIRCUS! I BEG YOU! I BEG YOU! PLEASE DO-!" *(mimics a chainsaw)* ERG-GR-GR-GR-GR-GR! *(acting as though he's getting attacked with a chainsaw)* "NO! I- DON'T! I BEG YOU!" ERG-GR-GR-GR-GR-GR! "AAAAAAAAAAAAAAAAAAAAAAAAA AAAAAAAAAAAAAAAAAAAAAAAAAAAAHHHHHH HHHHHHHHHHHHHHHHHHHHHHHHHHHHHHH!" *(he acts as though the chainsaw is dying whilst it is being plunged into him)* EEERG-GR-gr-gr-gr-gr-gr-gr-gr… gr-gr-gr… gr-gr… gr… gr…gr…

Doctor Circus then goes limp and lies on the dinner table as though he has died. Jane 1 and John look at him and then look at each other and then look back at him. Doctor Circus doesn't move.

JANE 1: *(whispering)* What is-

JOHN: *(whisper)* I don't know… *(to Doctor Circus)* Doc-I mean <u>Mister</u> Doctor Circus, are you alright?

Doctor Circus doesn't respond. He doesn't even move.

JOHN: *(to Jane 1)* I-

Doctor Circus shoots up, startling the couple. He then takes his seat, acting as though the large spectacle did not just take place. He looks at the couple as he takes a bite of the Bunyip before him.

DOCTOR CIRCUS: *(continuing what he was saying)* I think that it goes to show you that even those who devote their lives to teaching you that life after death will be eloquently wonderful, still have their doubts.

Doctor Circus looks at them as though he's just spoken words of wisdom. They look at him for a moment and then they look down at their food, which they have hardly eaten.

DOCTOR CIRCUS: *(motions to the food in front of his guests)* What's bothering you two? Don't you like the Bunyip?

They look at Doctor Circus and then down at their food again. It is clear they don't want to be rude, yet they are being rude by not speaking.

DOCTOR CIRCUS: *(standing)* DON'T YOU!!!

JOHN: Um, yes, it's just, well… We were coming home from dinner when we got in the accident.

JANE 1: Yeah, so I guess we're still pretty full.

DOCTOR CIRCUS: Well then, you must be tired.

JANE 1: Well now that you mention it…

DOCTOR CIRCUS: Well then, I will have Glee take you to your room. *(standing and shouting off)* Woe! Glee!

The two jesters reappear. Doctor Circus turns to Woe.

DOCTOR CIRCUS: Woe, will you please take the lady and her gentleman to their room? And be sure that you are as polite as you can be.

Woe nods as he clicks his heels and then looks to the couple. He motions for them to follow and then exits SL. The couple looks at each other and then to Doctor Circus.

JANE 1: Thank you for the food.

JOHN: Yeah, thank you.

DOCTOR CIRCUS: No, thank you for the company. May the two of you have a good night.

The couple smiles politely and then follows Woe OSL. Doctor Circus watches after them and then turns to Glee.

DOCTOR CIRCUS: Well aren't they just drab?

Glee nods, but does not say anything. Doctor Circus continues to look off, after the couple, a simple, inquisitive smile on his lips.

DOCTOR CIRCUS: That strapping young lad does seem promising though, no?

GLEE, THE WOEFUL: Sir, you can't be serious.

DOCTOR CIRCUS: Glee! How dare you! I am never serious! But I can't shake the feeling that he is oh-so right for what we need.

GLEE: Sir, I think-

DOCTOR CIRCUS: I don't care what you think, Glee! My word is law! You must prepare the house!

GLEE: Yes sir.

Doctor Circus and Glee exit SR. As they do this, all of the STAGEHANDS sweep the stage from SR to SL, dressing the set as though it were THE COUPLE'S BEDROOM, complete with two cots that are shaped like boxes. When they are done, Woe and the couple enter from SR. Woe bows and lets them enter before him. Once they're in there, looking around, Woe walks out of the OSR, leaving the two of them there to think. They look at each other and then sit on the two beds. All they can think to do is stare at each other, mouths agape.

JANE 1: I don't like this, John.

JOHN: I dunno, Jane, I think it's kind of cool, you know? In a weird way.

JANE 1: "Cool"? "Cool"?! That man is insane!

JOHN: What? You really think so? I think it's just an elaborate act. Like he's just getting a kick out of making us uncomfortable. He can't really be that way. He's just super lonely or something.

JANE 1: Well of course he's lonely, but don't you think that'd make someone a little nuts?

JOHN: I guess. I don't know. He's not really doing any harm. I think it's all just pretty entertaining.

JANE 1: *(stubborn, for some reason)* You think a man murdering a priest is entertaining, John?

JOHN: *(laughing)* Seriously, Jane? I don't think that man would actually kill a priest.

JANE 1: I don't know, John. I think if anyone would it would be that psychopath.

JOHN: Well why would he tell us about it if he did?

JANE 1: *(rhetorically)* Because he's insane?

DOCTOR CIRCUS: *(OS)* Hey now!

Doctor Circus storms in, his pointer finger raised angrily and pointing in the direction of Jane 1.

DOCTOR CIRCUS: Now that is just not fair, young lady.

JOHN: Doctor Circus, I-

DOCTOR CIRCUS: *(turning to John)* It's <u>Mister</u> Doctor Circus! *(back to Jane 1)* And you! How dare you!

JANE 1: I'm sorry, <u>Mister</u> Doctor Circus.

DOCTOR CIRCUS: *(condescending)* Oh are you? Ha! *(he sits down on the cot next to her)* I am not insane, my lady. Insanity is relative. Insanity is cause and effect! Insanity is good and bad! Insanity is everything, but it is not I! You see, madam, everyone is truly insane, by the oh-so simple definition of the word, yet it is those who embrace it that are the sane ones. It's those who realize this truth that can rise above it. *(putting his arm around Jane 1 as though she were his*

49

chum) So I ask you, madam! *(he stands and turns to Jane 1 with a look of smug satisfaction on his face)* Have I ever claimed to not be insane?

Doctor Circus looks as though he's about to snap as he stares Jane 1 down. Jane 1 doesn't meet his gaze however, she looks over to John and the two of them share an uncomfortable look.

DOCTOR CIRCUS: Well? Have I?

JANE 1: *(wishing that she could hide)* You just d-d-did, M-M-Mr. Doctor Circus...

DOCTOR CIRCUS: No, I assure you I did not.

JOHN: Actually sir, I'm pretty sure you just did.

Doctor Circus looks at the two of them for a moment, contemplatively, as though he's near his breaking point. He rubs the back of his neck, thinking.

DOCTOR CIRCUS: *(calling off)* Script!

Beat.

Glee and Woe walk out onto the stage with a SCRIPT in their hands.

DOCTOR CIRCUS: *(coldly looking at Jane 1)* We'll see about this! *(he rips the script from Glee and Woe's hands and begins to flip through it)* Let's see here... *(he continues to flip, not finding where they are)* Hmmm... *(turns to Glee)* What page are we on? *(Glee guides him through the script to the page where he begins to skim)* Ah, yes. *(mimicking John)* "Seriously, Jane? I don't really think the man would kill a priest." *(mocking John)* "The man," eh? I have a name, John, my boy. *(he scoffs and gets back to the script)* "It's not fair." Hmm-hmm-hmm. "I am not insane." Hmmm. Well there it is, right in black and white. *(he tosses the script over his shoulder and turns to Jane 1)* I guess I'm utterly mad! *(he cocks his head back and looks at Jane 1 as though he is, in fact, utterly mad)* How does it feel to be right, my dear?

Doctor Circus just stares Jane 1 down with a flicker of insanity in his eyes. She looks right back at him, a flicker of fear in hers.

JANE 1: So does that mean that you killed that man?

DOCTOR CIRCUS: Which man? The pauper? The prince? The butcher? The baker? The candlestick vendor? The liar? The priest? The flautist? Lincoln? The two strangers who got stranded and stayed the night at my house, spreading secrets and lies in the room I let them use so that they wouldn't get electrocuted by lightening? The ventriloquist? Which one?

JANE 1: T-the priest?

DOCTOR CIRCUS: Of course I killed that priest!

JANE 1: *(sounding judgmental)* Why on earth would you kill a man of the cloth?

DOCTOR CIRCUS: Because cloth is not armor and my blade was too sharp! You should always wear your armor to war, m'lady!

JOHN: "War"? What war?

DOCTOR CIRCUS: The War Against, my good man! It still rages on today. You aren't a liar, are you?

JOHN: *(fearing death)* No, no.

DOCTOR CIRCUS: I hope so, for your sake.

JANE 1: *(not being able to derail herself from the train of stubbornness she appears to be riding)* I just don't understand how you could kill anyone. Especially a priest. They are men of God.

DOCTOR CIRCUS: He was a liar, I assure you. There is no greater a liar than a priest, and I had to do it! All is fair in lust and war.

JANE 1: Don't you mean "lo-

DOCTOR CIRCUS: *(he extends his hand to clasp around her face and to squeeze her cheeks so very tightly that she can't open her mouth)* DON'T YOU DO IT! *(he leans into her, getting very close to her frightened face)* Did you not listen to my opening monologue?

JANE 1: *(through the squeezed cheeks and fear)* What?

DOCTOR CIRCUS: *(subduing his violent range for the time being)* Did you or did you not listen to the opening monologue?

Jane 1 just about pisses herself. Maybe she even does.

DOCTOR CIRCUS: *(growing impatient)* Well?

JANE 1: I did.

DOCTOR CIRCUS: So you're aware of the third rule of the house?

JOHN: *(correcting, for some reason, even though he knows what Doctor Circus meant)* It was the second rule.

DOCTOR CIRCUS: *(spins around to face John)* What!?

JOHN: It was rule number two. The one about the word you don't like.

DOCTOR CIRCUS: *(calm)* Oh yeah, that's right, I'm sorry. *(to Jane 1)* I'm sorry, I forgot. *(getting back into it)* So are you aware of the second rule of my house?

JANE 1: Yes.

DOCTOR CIRCUS: *(losing it)* THEN WHY WOULD YOU ALMOST MAKE THAT MISTAKE?! *(calming himself down)* Are you aware of the punishment? Or do you need to be told?

JANE 1: *(scared out of her wits)* Yes.

DOCTOR CIRCUS: Then why on earth would you do something like that?

JANE 1: I-I-I don't know.

DOCTOR CIRCUS: Because you're a brainless, dirty cunt[9]?

Jane 1 just looks at him, shaking with fear.

---

[9] Again, Doctor Circus has the upmost respect for women, but he is talking about the first Jane here, so it is justified to use this word.

DOCTOR CIRCUS: *(repeating himself in a condescending manner)* Is it because you're a brainless, dirty cunt[10], Jane? Hmm?

Again, Jane 1 says nothing.

DOCTOR CIRCUS: Say it, Jane.

Jane 1, for reasons only she understands, does not say it.

DOCTOR CIRCUS: *(at the end of his rope)* SAY THE GODDAMN LINE!

JANE 1: *(stammering)* I'm-I'm-I'm-

DOCTOR CIRCUS: YOU'RE WHAT JANE?! YOU'RE WHAT?!

JANE 1: *(blurting it out)* I'm a brainless, dirty cunt!

DOCTOR CIRCUS: *(very pleased)* Very good. *(he releases his grip on her face and let's her fall back onto her cot)* Now, for the matter at hand: *(he turns to face them both)* Before I was rudely interrupted while I was trying to eavesdrop on you, I was coming up here to give you some rather important information.

He stands there, not continuing. Jane 1 and John seem confused as to what's going on.

JANE 1: What were you going to tell us, Mister Doctor Circus?

---

[10] See Footnote 9.

DOCTOR CIRCUS: Oh, or course, yes. This reason I am here is because I feel it is my duty, as a good host, to notify you that morning will be postponed until further notice.

JOHN: Wait, what?

DOCTOR CIRCUS: YOU HEARD ME YOU SNIEVELING SWINE!

John shuts up, cowering a little bit. This makes Doctor Circus laugh a little chuckle.

DOCTOR CIRCUS: Now, I will be up to wake you for a meal whenever I find I am hungry. Have a goodnight, all.

With that he turns on his heels and marches out of the room OS, followed by Glee and Woe, who have just been standing there awkwardly the whole time. The couple is left there to stare at each other, as they are too afraid to speak until they are sure Doctor Circus is gone. They double check to make sure he has, indeed, left. Then John turns to Jane 1.

JOHN: What did he mean about postponing morning?

JANE 1: *(not wanting to speak to John)* I don't know.

JOHN: I mean he can't actually do that, right? I mean no one has that power.

DOCTOR CIRCUS: *(OS/ghost-like)* IIIIIIIIIIIIIIIII IIIIIIIIIIIIIIIIIIIIIIIII DDDDDDDDDDDDDDDDDD DDDDDDDDDDDDDDDDDDDDDDDDDDDDDDDDOO OOOOOOOOOOOOOOOOOOOOOOO!

55

John and Jane 1 look OS, a little creeped out, before John sits back down and looks over at Jane 1 who rolls away from him and sighs.

JOHN: What's wrong, babe[11]?

JANE 1: I don't want to talk about it, John.

JOHN: Oh, come on, Jane. Let's not do this now. What is bothering you?

JANE 1: *(she turns around angrily and faces him)* Where were you just now?

JOHN: What?

JANE 1: Where were you when that maniac was manhandling me?! Didn't it ever occur to you that you should defend your wife?

JOHN: I'm sorry, Jane; I wasn't thinking. I think I was just taken off guard.

JANE 1: Taken off guard? Taken off guard?! Do you think I wasn't taken off guard?!

JOHN: Jane, I'm sorry, babe[12]. I don't know what came over me, okay? I'm so glad you're okay, though, I'm sorry I wasn't there for you.

---

[11] If The Actress Playing "Jane" 1 is comely, she may be referred to as "honey" or, perhaps, "darling".

[12] See Footnote 11.

JANE 1: *(not satisfied with his answer)* Ugh, whatever.

Jane 1 rolls away from him. John lies on his back and sighs.

JANE 1: *(irritated by his sigh)* What, John?

JOHN: *(lying)* Nothing.

Jane 1 sighs, completely frustrated, and sits up, just looking at him.

JOHN: What, Jane?

JANE 1: Are you really going to do this?

JOHN: Do what?

JANE 1: The whole mope-y thing. You know you did something wrong, right?

JOHN: I was afraid, Jane! I couldn't even process what was happening!

JANE 1: Oh you were afraid, huh? That shouldn't even matter! How do you think the love of your li- *(realizes what she just said)* Oh shit!

DOCTOR CIRCUS: *(OS)* WHAT IS THE SECOND FUCKING RULE?!

John now realizes what is happening just as Doctor Circus storms on stage, an AXE in his hand. He brings it down onto Jane 1's head.

JOHN: NO!

Doctor Circus brings the axe down one more time on Jane 1.

DOCTOR CIRCUS *(to Jane 1)* I just fucking told you! *(to the stagehands OS)* CUT THE GODDAMN LIGHTS!

The lights are cut and the sounds of someone being axed to death[13] are all that can be heard. Suddenly it stops.

DOCTOR CIRCUS: *(from the darkness)* Someone clean this wench[14] up!

The sound of the axe being thrown on the stage can be heard.

DOCTOR CIRCUS: *(loudly)* CURTAINS!

The curtains can be heard closing.

END ACT I.

---

[13] If you are unsure what this sounds like, listen to the wailing of a raccoon caught in a bear trap while you chop a tomato that you've placed on top of half an onion with a cleaver that has not been sharpened in awhile.

[14] See Footnote 4 or 9 (or even 10)

RANT II

A few seconds pass and Doctor Circus walks out from underneath the closed curtains. He stomps his cane down and a spotlight shines on him. He is covered in blood.

DOCTOR CIRCUS: *(barely tries to clean himself up)* I'm sorry, my friends, that you had to experience that. But if there is one thing I am, it's a stickler for the rules. *(he laughs)* So yes, we've found ourselves in an unfortunate situation. But not to fear! That is why we have back up plans! I knew this Jane was weak and so plans were set in motion to ensue that even if this happened, the show could go on seamlessly. *(laughs again, it seems like it is only to himself for he is the only man, woman or child that seems to find his humor funny)* "Seamlessly". The show was going so well, don't you think? *(no answer, hopefully, if there is an answer from the audience they are to be removed posthaste at Doctor Circus's behest)* DON'T YOU?! Ah, what do you know anyway? This shit, this shit, how it's all for you and yet, and yet, there is nothing you so do for me. *(he just stands there now, looking off into the distance, passed the audience and into the world behind them all)* A play is what they wanted and a play is what they shall receive! *(he perks up)* So yes! On with the show as they say! Let us all commence! Before we do so, however, there is a note. The part of "Jane" shall now be played by *[insert the actress playing Actress Playing "Jane" 2's name]*. And the show shall continue without further interruption. At least that is the hope.

He goes to move back under the curtains when he appears to be stopped by someone trying to get his attention OS.

DOCTOR CIRCUS: *(looking OS)* What? *(he gets an unheard response from OS)* Oh, alright. They aren't going to like it, but if you say so. *(he turns back to face the audience)* So, it appears –and I am sorry about this, my friends- that we are running a little long tonight. So in order to save on time, intermission is cancelled this evening. I hope that this isn't too big of an inconvenience on all of you seemingly nice people.

Doctor Circus then does something that can only be described as a "sarcastic bow" (it is sarcastic, because why on earth should he bow down to the swine that are sitting in front of him, hanging on his every word.) before he crawls back under the curtain.

END RANT II.

ACT II

The curtains open and the lights come up. We're back in the bedroom. John is sitting on the bed where he was previously sitting. THE ACTRESS PLAYING "JANE" 2 sits where the original Jane sat before, what will be described for years to come as, "the incident". Doctor Circus stands between them. They are all looking at a copy of the script. He looks up when he notices the lights are on and the audience is looking at him. He realizes he needs to get on with the show.

DOCTOR CIRCUS: *(quietly, to himself and his cast)* So we're clear on the changes?

JOHN: *(in shock/quietly)* Yeah.

JANE 2: *(excited to be there/quietly)* Sounds good to me.

DOCTOR CIRCUS: Okay, so we'll take it from the "swine" bit?

John and Jane 2 acknowledge it's a good call. Doctor Circus gets into character, as does Jane 2 (she cares about this roll more than whoever played Jane 1). Doctor Circus moves over to John, who is in shock, still, but comes out of it quickly when he sees Doctor Circus standing over him in a rage.

DOCTOR CIRCUS: *(he puts his finger in John's face)* YOU HEARD ME YOU SNIEVELING SWINE!

John cowers a bit, half in character, half out.

DOCTOR CIRCUS: *(calming himself)* Now, I will be up to wake you for a meal whenever I discover that I've grown hungry. Now, please, sleep well, you two.

With that he turns on his heels and marches out of the room, without Glee and Woe this time around (they were never on stage). The couple is left there to stare at one another. They're too afraid to speak until they are sure that Doctor Circus is out of earshot. They check to make sure he's gone before John turns to Jane 2. [It should be noted that John always cares for Jane 2 more than he cared for Jane 1. It seems like the only reason he even feigned interest in Jane 1 was so that he could spare Jane 2. But, we'll never be sure, this is all just how it seemed.

JOHN: What do you think he meant by "postponing morning"?

JANE 2: *(not wanting to speak to John)* I don't know.

JOHN: I mean, he can't do that, right? I mean no one has that power.

DOCTOR CIRCUS: *(OS/ghost-like)* IIIIIIIIIIIIIIIII IIIIIIIIIIIIIIIIIIIIIIIIII DDDDDDDDDDDDDDDDDD DDDDDDDDDDDDDDDDDDDDDDDDDDDDDDDDDD DDDDDDDDDDDDDDDDOOOOOOOOOOOOOOOOO OOOOOOOOOOOOOOOOOOO!

They look OS, a little creeped out, before John sits back down and looks over at Jane 2, who rolls away from him and sighs.

JOHN: Are you alright?

JANE 2: Am I alright? Are you crazy? Or course I'm not alright! I was just manhandled, and you just sat there like some sort of dolt!

JOHN: Jane, baby, it's all part of this plan that I have. I've just come up with it. It's a good one.

JANE 2: *(raising her voice slightly)* Oh, you are so full of it!

JOHN: Shhhh! *(whispering)* Look, don't you want to get out of here?

JANE 2: Of course I want to get out of here! I've wanted out since we got here. You're the one who seems like they want to stay.

JOHN: No, of course I don't want to stay. I just figure that if we're to get out of here we should be on Mr. Doctor Circus's good side. So all you have to do is keep acting like you're acting, then I'll keep acting like I'm acting, and maybe he'll trust me or like me or something and then we'll be able to get out of here. It's just very important that he doesn't catch on. I need to play dumb.

Jane 2 just looks at him, a smirk upon her face.

JOHN: What?

JANE 2: You're a genius.

JOHN: Well I do try.

JANE 2: I like this idea a lot, but do you think it will really work?

JOHN: *(shudders before insult/hushed)* Doctor Circus is a pompous asshole. *(un-hushed)* I know this will work as long as I continue to play into his psychotic whims.

JANE 2: Well I have faith in you. Just don't get caught up, okay? You know how you get.

JOHN: I won't, my dear, don't worry. Now, if only I could see what he's up to now...

As though it were kismet sent from above, Glee and Woe enter and stand at attention before them.

GLEE, THE WOEFUL: Doctor Circus is requesting your presence.

WOE, THE GLEEFUL: And please do hurry, time is of the essence.

JOHN: Okay, but *(he winks to Jane 2, in a rather over-exaggerated fashion)* it should just be me, though. My wife isn't feeling well.

WOE, THE GLEEFUL: We cannot lie; that is most likely best.

GLEE, THE WOEFUL: If your wife is ill, she should probably rest.

JOHN: Very good. *(to Jane 2)* I'll see you in awhile. *(back to Glee and Woe)* Shall we go?

GLEE and WOE: Of course.

They exit SR and John follows giving Jane 2 a reassuring signal. As they exit, the STAGEHANDS enter in a wave SL, and dress the stage so that it looks like THE HOUSE OF BOXES PARLOR. There's a bar and a fireplace. Doctor Circus's chair is placed next to it and they exit SR. Doctor Circus enters and sits in his chair. There's a beat and then John is escorted in SL, by Glee and Woe, who exit promptly after delivering John. John stands there for a while; it appears as though Doctor Circus has not noticed John.

JOHN: Um… Doctor Circus.

DOCTOR CIRCUS: <u>Mister</u>.

JOHN: Um, <u>Mister</u> Circus.

DOCTOR CIRCUS: No, <u>Mister</u> Doctor Circus. *(explaining)* Dr. Doctor Circus was my father's name. He never let me forget it.

JOHN: Oh, I- uh –see. Well, <u>Mister</u> Doctor Circus, I'm here to see you, as you requested.

DOCTOR CIRCUS: Aren't we all?

JOHN: Excuse me?

DOCTOR CIRCUS: Pardon?

JOHN: What?

DOCTOR CIRCUS: Indeed.

Doctor Circus rises. John instinctively steps back from the superior being, a little afraid. He trips, slightly and this makes Doctor Circus laugh.

JOHN: Sorry.

DOCTOR CIRCUS: Don't be. *(he begins to pour himself a drink from the bar)* Jonah, I-

JOHN: John.

DOCTOR CIRCUS: *(snappy)* What!?

JOHN: My name is John, sir.

DOCTOR CIRCUS: You will be whatever I name you, damn it!

JOHN: I'm-

DOCTOR CIRCUS: You are beyond nothing, you understand?! Nothing! Not without me! Not without my words! Are you not clear of this fact of facts?

JOHN: No, sir, I know that, I just thought-

DOCTOR CIRCUS: You thought! Ha! That would be the day. I can't believe the audacity you have! That's no way for a "Jonah" to behave. An "Ian" maybe, but a "Jonah"? Never.

JOHN: You're right, sir, I'm sorry.

DOCTOR CIRCUS: You damn well better be! Now John, do you know why it is that I've called you hear?

JOHN: No. Should I know?

DOCTOR CIRCUS: Perhaps. It depends on who you ask.

JOHN: What do you mean?

DOCTOR CIRCUS: I mean what I say! Don't you understand that yet?

He stares John down. John doesn't move.

JOHN: *(not knowing what to do)* Um...

DOCTOR CIRCUS: *(oddly calm)* I abhor stupidity, John. It's the worst of all traits. We all know it too, this pathetic species of ours. Yet, we coddle it, for some reason I will never understand. If we're not careful, we'll end up being run by a buffoon like you. *(a realization dawns on him)* Do you know what, my boy?

JOHN: What?

DOCTOR CIRCUS: I think this might be the calmest I've ever been. *(he looks to John with a serine smile on his face)* Perhaps your stupidity brings it out in me. When my superiority is evident, it makes me calm, it seems.

JOHN: *(trying to seem agreeable)* Yes sir.

DOCTOR CIRCUS: *(snapping out of serenity)* DON'T YOU FUCKING PATRONIZE ME YOU CUNTY EXCUSE FOR A TWAT! *(he approaches John, who cowers immediately)* I AM THE PHALLUS THAT KEEPS YOU IN CHECK AND YOU ARE THAT THING BETWIXT YOUR WIFE'S LEGS! I AM NOT SOME LIMP PROTUBERANCE, LIKE YOU AND YOUR FATHER'S BEFORE YOU! *(he now finds himself right in John's stupid face)* JUST ASK YOUR MOTHER! *(he pushes John over and stands above him, yelling down)* ASK YOUR WHORE OF A MOTHER!

JOHN: *(too scared to talk)* I- I- I- My- My- My- My- Sh- Sh-

DOCTOR CIRCUS: WHAT!?

JOHN: *(blurting it out)* My mother is dead, sir! *(calmer)* She has passed on.

DOCTOR CIRCUS: *(instantaneously drops the anger completely)* Haven't we all? *(he extends his hand to John so that he can help him to his feet)* Get up, my boy. The floor is no place for a grown man. *(seeing John's reluctance)* Come on, now; don't be frightened.

John takes his hand and is heaved up. Doctor Circus goes back to the bar and grabs his drink. John just stands there, still wary of all that has just transpired. Doctor Circus takes a sip of his drink and looks at John. Absolutely nothing is said between them for quite some time. Doctor Circus just stares at John, trying to size him up, John stares back, not knowing what to do. It is apparent that John is made uncomfortable by Doctor Circus's gaze.

JOHN: Um… is everything alright, sir?

DOCTOR CIRCUS: Say your line, John.

JOHN: What?

DOCTOR CIRCUS: Say your goddamn line.

JOHN: It isn't my line, sir.

DOCTOR CIRCUS: What? Is it mine?

JOHN: Yes.

DOCTOR CIRCUS: Oh, silly me. *(thinks about it)* I have no idea where we are. *(calling off)* LINE! *(he listens off stage, but can't hear)* WHAT?! *(calms down)* I really can't hear a thing that you're saying.

Woe scurries on stage and whispers to Doctor Circus. He nods to whatever he's being told.

DOCTOR CIRCUS: Okay, thank you.

Woe does a little bow and then scurries back off stage.

DOCTOR CIRCUS: *(turning to John/back in character)* So, John, do you know why I called you here?

JOHN: No sir, I have no idea.

DOCTOR CIRCUS: Well, it's all rather simple, really. I've called you here so that I can ask you one question. Just one. This question will lead to more questions and then hopefully we will find ourselves in the midst of what I call a "conversation". Then, hopefully, the petty pleasantries associated with "conversation" will drift away and we'll find ourselves deep in the depths of a deep and true dialogue. Would that be alright with you? I know it could be a lot to ask of someone that you've just met.

JOHN: Whatever you say, Mr. Doctor Circus.

DOCTOR CIRCUS: *(pouring another drink in a separate glass)* Mr. Doctor Circus was my grandfather; please, call me Doctor Circus, The Great. *(handing the drink he's poured to John)* Now, it's time for the big question, the question on everyone's mind. Are you ready for it John?

JOHN: Yes, sir, I believe I am.

DOCTOR CIRCUS: Are you sure about that?

JOHN: Yes.

DOCTOR CIRCUS: Are you absolutely, one-hundred percent positive?

JOHN: Yes, sir, please ask me anything.

DOCTOR CIRCUS: Oh, I will.

Before Doctor Circus speaks, he clinks his glass on John's, points OS, and, when John looks in the direction of his finger, he pours something into John's drink. He then takes a big swig from his drink, finishing the whole thing in one gulp. He throws the cup over his shoulder and it clanks on the floor. He stares at John until John drinks his own drink, not breaking his gaze until John is done. When John finishes, Doctor Circus gives him a little applause.

DOCTOR CIRCUS: So John, we would all like to know: How complete is your devotion to your wife, exactly?

JOHN: *(taken aback)* Oh. *(deciding how to answer)* Well I do like her a whole lot. She is just about my favorite person on this whole planet.

DOCTOR CIRCUS: *(finding this trite)* So she's the "bee's knees" then, is she?

JOHN: Oh yes sir.

DOCTOR CIRCUS: *(dour)* Well that makes this all the more difficult then, doesn't it?

JOHN: What more difficult?

DOCTOR CIRCUS: Oh, have we not gotten there yet?

JOHN: No, I don't think so.

DOCTOR CIRCUS: Oh, well, silly me, again. *(laughing and going to the bar, pouring another drink)* Do you know how to use a sword, John?

JOHN: What?

DOCTOR CIRCUS: *(sipping his drink)* Oh, do you not know what a sword is?

JOHN: No, I know what a sword is. I just don't think I look like the type of per-

At this moment, and without any warning whatsoever, the Person from the Audience, from before, runs out from OS, tripping over something and falling to the floor. They are bloody and have remnants of rope around them. It looks as though one of their eyes has been removed from their head, but you can't be sure. It's a bloody mess around there.

PERSON FROM THE AUDIENCE: *(calling out to anyone)* Oh god, please help me!

DOCTOR CIRCUS: *(looking at The Person with disgust)* God damnit, can someone grab them please?!

Without thought, John grabs The Person and holds them tightly. Glee and Woe run onto the stage and join John. The three of them wrestle the Person from the Audience to the ground.

PERSON FROM THE AUDIENCE: *(to the audience, maybe)* They killed that girl! They killed that girl and said I'm nex-

DOCTOR CIRCUS: DAMN IT ALL! HOLD THAT NUISANCE STILL!

Doctor Circus approaches quickly, pulling out his knife and crouching to the Person's level.

PERSON FROM THE AUDIENCE: *(to John, Glee, and Woe)* Please, someone, stop him!

Doctor Circus brings down the dagger. The Person lets out a blood curdling scream and then all is deathly quiet.

Beat.

Doctor Circus rises, wiping the blood off the dagger on his pants, it just adds to the milieu. He turns to face the audience.

DOCTOR CIRCUS: *(directly to the audience)* I guess we're all in this together. *(to Glee and Woe)* Clean this mess.

Glee, Woe, and John hoist the body up and go to move it OS with less hassle than one might think.

DOCTOR CIRCUS: Not you, John, you stay with me.

JOHN: *(reluctantly looking at Glee, Woe, and the body)* Alright.

John helps Glee and Woe get situated with the body and then watches them move the body OS. As this transpires, Doctor Circus goes to the bar and pours himself a drink. He downs it immediately and then pours another. He downs this one as well and then pours yet another. He repeats until the body is completely clear from view. Once it's done, he pours a final drink, not drinking it, as he turns to face John.

DOCTOR CIRCUS: *(he smirks a large smirk)* Alright then, now where were we? *(he thinks, then:)* Oh yes: the art of the sword! How familiar are you with it?

JOHN: Not very. Not at all, really. I can't recall if I've ever even held a sword before.

DOCTOR CIRCUS: Ha! How droll. I was the exact same way before all of this happened. Before the boxes. Before the hat. I was a chess man, myself, before all of this. Do you know how to play chess, at least?

JOHN: I have before. I am not very good at it.

DOCTOR CIRCUS: Well practice makes perfect, my boy. Although, for you, that point might be moot.

JOHN: *(slightly offended)* I don't know if I like the sound of that.

DOCTOR CIRCUS: I suppose that makes you smarter than I thought you were. Probably smarter than anyone thought you were. There may be some hope for you yet. Even if it is just a sliver.

JOHN: Hope for what?

Doctor Circus looks over at John, that wonderfully devilish smile grows across his face.

DOCTOR CIRCUS: Are you a fan of hats, John?

JOHN: *(thinking about it)* Yes?

DOCTOR CIRCUS: What do you think of my hat? I'm, personally quite fond of it.

JOHN: That is a mighty fine hat.

DOCTOR CIRCUS: Could you ever see yourself wearing it?

JOHN: I don't know about that.

DOCTOR CIRCUS: Would you like to wear it?

JOHN: *(uncomfortable, for some reason)* Oh, I definitely don't know about <u>that</u>. It looks very good on you.

DOCTOR CIRCUS: *(smirking at the flattery)* That it does. But what would you do if I told you that it could give you all the power that you could ever desire?

JOHN: *(laughing uncomfortably)* I don't deserve too much, Mr. Doc- I mean Doctor Circus, The Gre-

DOCTOR CIRCUS: Oh, you have no idea what you desire.

JOHN: *(laughing, again uncomfortably)* Yeah, I get that a lot.

DOCTOR CIRCUS: *(snapping)* This isn't a joke! *(he downs his drink and throws the cup away)* Do you realize what you are capable of?! *(kind of ticking)* Do you? Do you? Do you? DO you? Do YOU? DO YOU? *(approaches a worried John)* DO YOU?! DO YOU?! *(standing in front of John/different inflection)* DO YOU?! DO YOU?! DO YOU?! DO YOU?! *(he loses it and flails about, it seems as though he might be broken)* DO YOU! DO YOU! DO YOU! DO YOU! DO YOU! DO YOU! DO YOU! *(he now seems a little afraid)* DO Y-Y-YOU?!

As he continues to be trapped in his "Do You's" He motions OS and Glee and Woe rush out. One carries a BROWN BOTTLE,

the other a SYRINGE. Memory doesn't allow for a clear picture of who had what, so this can be made up.

DOCTOR CIRCUS: DO! YOU! DO! YOU! DO! YOU! DO! YOU! DO! YOU! *(grabs the syringe from whom ever has it and prepares the syringe as though he has done this a million times before)* DO? YOU! DO? YOU! DO? YOU! DO? YOU! *(he injects himself, the effects of which are nearly instantaneous)* DO! YOU? DO! You? Do you? do... *(he slumps onto the floor)* Do... You... Do... You... Do... You... *(he exhales deeply)* I hate when this happens. *(He then looks over to John while still sitting on the floor)* So... Do you, John? Do you realize your full potential?

JOHN: I- I really don't know.

DOCTOR CIRCUS: *(rising)* Well you should figure that out. *(to Glee and Woe)* I'm okay now, thank you. You can go about your business. Or my business as it were. Be gone.

Glee and Woe exit the stage.

DOCTOR CIRCUS: *(turning back to John)* You're a sniveling dolt, John, but you don't need to be. *(he goes to the bar and pours himself another drink)* You know, John, all that you could ever want could be yours if you take this hat from atop my head and put it on to yours. If you wished to attempt such a feat, there would be a fight, however. That much you should know.

JOHN: I really don't want to fight you, Doctor Circus, The Great.

DOCTOR CIRCUS: No one ever wants to fight. No one. Ever. But sometimes you need to and most times you have to and if you don't it's the regret, not the cowardice, that will do you in. You understand what I am saying to you?

JOHN: Well, I really don't like feeling regret.

DOCTOR CIRCUS: *(chipper)* Good. *(walks over to John in a friendly manner)* So what do you say, John? Do you fancy a duel for my hat?

JOHN: I-

Doctor Circus puts his finger on John's lips.

DOCTOR CIRCUS: And before you answer, John, know this: This moment here, this is the most important part of the play. Your answer could bring on the grand and epic finale the audience arguably deserves, or it could lead to more boring droning. It's more than you and your needs that you must consider. This is all bigger than you.

JOHN: I know that. I just- I mean my wife? I think I should talk to Jane about this.

DOCTOR CIRCUS: Oh yes, your dear wife. How could I have forgotten such an important character in all of this? You're absolutely right about being concerned with that. You should most assuredly talk to her before you make your mind up; I know how important the opinions of the fairer sex can be, especially to folks like you and I. You should know this, though John: No matter what your decision is, whether you decide to duel or not, she will not make it out of this house alive. The only person you stand to save with this decision is yourself, and only yourself.

JOHN: *(believing he must have misheard)* Did you just-

DOCTOR CIRCUS: Now, now, now. Tut, tut, tut. Save your words for that tempting wife of yours. That's enough of a dialogue for the night. *(calling off)* Glee! Woe!

Glee and Woe enter.

DOCTOR CIRCUS: *(to John)* Go talk to your wife. Come and see me when you are done with her. *(to Glee and Woe)* Take him to his room.

With that, Doctor Circus turns on his heels and exits SR. All John can do is look after him. He then turns to Glee and Woe, looking like he is trapped in a state of disbelief as he attempts to process what all has just transpired.

GLEE, THE WOEFUL: Are you ready to put yourself to bed?

WOE, THE GLEEFUL: You look weary; you should rest your head.

JOHN: Um, yeah, okay.

Glee and Woe exit SL. As soon as they're clear off the stage, the STAGEHANDS enter SR and transform the set from the lair back to THE BEDROOM. Jane 2 is with them and lies down on her bed as soon as the stage is set.

Beat.

Glee and Woe enter SR, followed closely by John.

WOE, THE GLEEFUL: Hopefully a good night is in store for you.

GLEE, THE WOEFUL: Yes, please sleep well. We now bid you adieu.

Glee and Woe bow slightly and then exit.

John watches after them and then looks at the sleeping Jane 2.

JOHN: Jane? *(he approaches her, nudging her gently)* Jane?

Jane 2 stirs and looks at John.

JANE 2: John? Is that you? How was the meeting with Doctor?

JOHN: *(not beating around the bush)* Jane, we have to leave.

JANE 2: What?

JOHN: *(sternly)* We have to leave right now.

JANE 2: John, you're scaring me.

JOHN: I can't lose you again.

JANE 2: *(trying not to break character)* Heh. I don't know what that means, John.

JOHN: *(ignoring this)* He's crazy. And he's getting even crazier. Very crazy. He said-

John begins to sob in his hands. Jane 2 leans up and comforts him as best she can.

JANE 2: John, darling, what happened?

JOHN: *(looking up at her/ overly serious)* You're going to die here, Jane.

JANE 2: Wha-

JOHN: He wants me to fight him for his hat. I don't know why or wha- It doesn't matter. What he said was however the fight ended up, whether I win or he wins, no matter the outcome, you wouldn't be leaving this place alive. *(he looks at Jane 2 with all the sincerity in the world)* We have to leave right this minute.

JANE 2: Okay.

JOHN: *(standing)* Find a weapon, I'm going to check the hall.

JANE 2: *(looking at the boxes)* Uh, okay.

John, exits. Jane 2 gets up and begins to look through the boxes. In the first box she finds POTATOES and OLD HARDCOVER BOOKS. She moves to the second box; it is full of WOMEN'S LINGERIE and RANDOM BITS OF MEAT. She holds up one of the bits before she is utterly disgusted by it and throws it back into the box. She then moves on to a third one; it's nothing but STUFFED ANIMALS and GAS MASKS. Finally she moves to the forth, the penultimate box in the room, and opens it. Inside this one there is BUBBLE WRAP, PACKING PEANUTS, and A HATCHET. She holds it up, triumphantly.

JANE 2: *(calling off)* John! *(she waits for John to answer, but she doesn't get any, this makes her worried)* John?

Jane 2 tiptoes SR and looks OS. She sees what is happening, gasps, and backs away. Glee and Woe enter SR, holding a struggling John.

JOHN: Let go of me!

JANE 2: *(concerned)* John! Are you okay?

JOHN: I'm fine. *(to Woe and Glee)* You better let me go!

GLEE, THE WOEFUL: If that happened, Doctor Circus would not be pleased.

WOE, THE GLEEFUL: Yes, dear sister, this is the last thing he needs.

JOHN: You don't have to tell him, you know. You can come with us. We can all get out of here.

JANE 2: Yes, come with us. Surely you can't be happy here.

WOE, THE GLEEFUL: You fools; happiness is not the issue.

GLEE, THE WOEFUL: We're to serve the master, no mat-

John thrusts his way out of their grasps. He punches Glee to the floor and grabs Woe, getting him in a choke-hold. He looks to Jane 2 and extends his non-choke-holding hand.

JOHN: Throw me the hatchet!

JANE 2: John, I-

JOHN: Jane, now!

JANE 2: Let him go!

JOHN: No! They're as crazy as him, maybe even crazier. Throw me the damn hatchet!

JANE 2: John, I don't think-

Woe bites John's hand. He cries out and without a hint of hesitation he snaps Woe's neck with a loud crack. He stands and the body drops. Without thinking, he goes to Woe.

JANE 2: *(shocked, maybe even disgusted)* John, I-

JOHN: *(staring her down)* They'll never stop, Jane. We can stop all this now. We can-

Glee, who has come to from the powerful blow John gave her, grabs John's leg.

WOE, THE GLEEFUL: You bastard! You killed my-

John kicks her with his free leg and then straddles her violently as Glee flails about.

JANE 2: Stop it, John! Stop!

John doesn't stop. He keeps strangling and strangling and strangling while Glee tries to escape. Finally, John gets forceful with it, shaking Glee about, until at last, Glee goes limp. John sits there for awhile, catching his breath. He then stands and turns to Jane 2.

JANE 2: *(staring down at Glee's body)* Is she...?

JOHN: Yes. I had to, Jane. *(he goes to try and comfort her, but she retracts from him)* Jane, don't. I know you're new to all of this, but this is how it goes. If I didn't slay them now, they'd come back at the end and thwart our escape.

JANE 2: John, you are scaring me. I don't know what you're talking about.

JOHN: Jane, we can talk about this later. Right now we need to go.

As he says this the box that Jane 2 did not go through bursts open. Doctor Circus rises from it and looks at them.

DOCTOR CIRCUS: You're not going anywhere you sorry excuse for a biped!

Jane 2 and John whip around and see Doctor Circus. They are taken by surprise. Doctor Circus just laughs and strides over to John before John has a chance to say anything. He knocks him out with his cane. He then pulls out his dagger and goes to Jane 2.

JANE 2: No, don't! Please! I'm preg-

He jams the knife into her gut, silencing her.

DOCTOR CIRCUS: Not anymore, you're not. *(to the back of the house)* Cut the fucking lights! *(once the lights are cut)* Draw the curtains and set the stage!

He walks up to the apron as the curtains close behind him.

END ACT II.

RANT III

A spotlight shines on Doctor Circus as he stands CS in front of the closed curtains. He looks rather sullen, almost depressed even, as he wipes the blood from his dagger and puts it back where he keeps it.

DOCTOR CIRCUS: *(shaking his head)* My friends, my friends, my friends. What am I to do? Well first, I suppose I would like to have a moment of silence for my fallen comrades. Glee... Oh Glee... You were the daughter I never had, the sister I never desired... And Woe! Oh, Woe how could he? You were so young. You were nothing more than a brother to me, perhaps a close cousin even. You were also nothing less than a mere acquaintance. I know I was known to say worse at times, but I hope you know now, in death, that my sternness was only an attempt to make you stronger. And how strong you two became! You were both strong. You were both the light of my lives. You were a ballast on the ship of my mind. You were two shining beacons of light in the night. A dark, dark, stormy night. The night was made darker by the beacon's existence. The beacons that exploited the empty void. Pushing me down, down, down, until there is no more. How will I ever have that again? How in the world will I ever find companionship such as that? *(thinking about it)* I could always make more, I suppose. But this batch- this batch in particular. This batch was superb. Undoubtedly so. Perhaps John and Jane will do? *(thinks about this)* No. No... Jane has to die. Especially now. That twat of a cunt. And John. Fucking John. He has to pay and pay and pay. Oh! Speaking of...

Doctor Circus stomps his cane on the floor and waits. Soon a stomp is heard behind the curtain. This stomp is a signal.

DOCTOR CIRCUS: Alright, very good. Let's get back to the show, eh? I'm excited to see where it goes. *(calling off)* Curtains!

The curtains start to open and the spotlight turns off as Doctor Circus begins to walk onto the stage.

END RANT III

ACT III

The curtains are fully up and Doctor Circus is walking to the middle of the stage. Silhouettes of how the stage is set can be seen, but the audience shouldn't be able to get a full view of it quite yet.

DOCTOR CIRCUS: Can I get the lights?

The lights come up and the audience gets to see a setting they have yet to see. It is the HOUSE OF BOXES BOX ROOM. All of the boxes are out on stage, it looks haphazard. In the middle of the metaphorical sea of boxes, and in full view of the audience, lies Jane 2. She is bleeding from her stomach. Down in LSR we have John, who is tied to a chair. He is still unconscious and appears to have quite the wound on his head. Doctor Circus approaches him and shakes him a bit. John doesn't stir in the slightest. Doctor Circus groans at this and goes to a box. On his way there, he crosses by Jane 2. She reaches out to him, desperately. He steps away from her, in disgust, and goes to a box toward the back of the stage. He opens it and it's filled with PANTRY DISHES and BALLS OF YARN. He digs through it, throwing things hither and tither. At last, at the very bottom, he reaches what he was looking for, an EMPTY WATER PITCHER. He grips it with excitement and heads back down stage. He crosses by Jane 2, again, on the way back down. She reaches out for a second time. This time Doctor Circus lunges towards her, as though he is about to hit her. She flinches away and he laughs maniacally. He makes his way to the next box. It is filled with some sort of BROWN LIQUID and A VARIETY OF SPORTS BALLS. He throws a FOOTBALL out from it and then dips the pitcher into the liquid and pulls it out, full. There's a BILLIARD BALL in the pitcher, which Doctor Circus plucks out and throws back into the box before he shuts the lid. He then crosses back over to John, walking carefully, so as not to spill a single drop of the precious liquid. He then stands before John, positioning himself, dramatically, as though he is about to douse John with the pitcher's contents.

DOCTOR CIRCUS: Are you ready to wake up, John?

He splashes John with the pitcher's contents. John shoots awake, screaming bloody murder. This makes Doctor Circus laugh very, very hard.

DOCTOR CIRCUS: Did you have a nice rest?

JOHN: What are you planning to do with us?

DOCTOR CIRCUS: Wouldn't you like to know?

JOHN: What the hell is wrong with you, man?

DOCTOR CIRCUS: *(laughing)* Haven't we been over this already?

JOHN: Won't you please just let us go?

DOCTOR CIRCUS: *(referencing the previous questions)* What the hell is wrong with you?

JOHN: *(nearly losing it)* Where's Jane? What have you done to her? Is she dead? Did you kill her, you murderous bastard?

DOCTOR CIRCUS: And just what, pray tell, would you do if I already had?

JOHN: I'd tell you I'd kill you, but you would like that, wouldn't you?

DOCTOR CIRCUS: You think you know me so well, do you?

JOHN: *(beaten down)* Why do you insist on playing these games?

DOCTOR CIRCUS: Can I ask you a question?

JOHN: Isn't that all we've been doing?

DOCTOR CIRCUS: *(ignoring John's inanity)* Did you know she was pregnant?

JOHN: *(taken aback)* Who? Jane?

DOCTOR CIRCUS: Who else would I be referring to?

JOHN: Jane is pregnant?

DOCTOR CIRCUS: *(to the audience)* Would it be mean if I corrected his "is" to "was"?

John lets out a rather pathetic sob at hearing this.

DOCTOR CIRCUS: So you didn't know?

JOHN: Do I ever know?

DOCTOR CIRCUS: Do you think we can stick to the script, please?

John shakes of some sort of inner turmoil that seems rather pathetic, but perhaps the audience can relate to it.

JOHN: H-how could I have known?

DOCTOR CIRCUS: She didn't tell you?

JOHN: Did she know?

Doctor Circus doesn't respond, he just sniggers a little bit and looks at John with a smile of pure elation.

JOHN: Did she know, Doctor Circus?

DOCTOR CIRCUS: *(shrugs)* How about we ask her?

Doctor Circus turns and walks to Jane 2, kneeling next to her.

DOCTOR CIRCUS: *(gently grabbing Jane 2's face)* Did you know?

JANE 2: *(in pain)* Why are you doing this?

DOCTOR CIRCUS: Why aren't you? *(laughing/turning to John)* See, what did I tell you?

JOHN: *(almost pleading)* Was she really pregnant?

DOCTOR CIRCUS: Shouldn't you know?

JOHN: How could I know?

DOCTOR CIRCUS: Couldn't you smell it on her?

JOHN: What?

DOCTOR CIRCUS: Couldn't you smell your spawn's sweet stench eking out of her sorry excuse for a cunt?

JOHN: What the fuck are you, you monster?

DOCTOR CIRCUS: Would you really like to know?

JOHN: Are you going to ask me to duel you again?

DOCTOR CIRCUS: *(rhetorical)* When did I become so predictable? *(to John/seriously)* What would you say if I did ask you to duel me now?

JOHN: Haven't you understood that I will never duel you?

DOCTOR CIRCUS: *(genuinely)* Aw, John, why won't you ever fight me?

JOHN: Why would I give you what you want?

DOCTOR CIRCUS: Whatever do you mean, <u>John</u>?

JOHN: Why would I give you the satisfaction of killing me?

DOCTOR CIRCUS: Don't you think that if I wanted to kill you, that you'd already be dead?

JOHN: Well then why would I give you the satisfaction of dying by my hand?

DOCTOR CIRCUS: You honestly think that would be the outcome?

JOHN: Then what is it you want, Doctor Circus?

DOCTOR CIRCUS: Didn't I already tell you to call me <u>Mister</u> Doctor Circus?

JOHN: Then what do you want, <u>Mister</u> Doctor Circus?

DOCTOR CIRCUS: Don't you already know?

JOHN: Do you want me to watch you kill Jane?

DOCTOR CIRCUS: *(laughing)* Are you really such a dolt that you don't understand any of this?

JOHN: *(dejected)* Why won't you just tell me what you want?

DOCTOR CIRCUS: Where would be the fun in that?

JOHN: *(sadly)* Why won't you just kill me?

DOCTOR CIRCUS: Do you think it could be that easy?

JOHN: *(pleading)* Won't you just kill me, please?

John hangs his head in a sign of surrender.

DOCTOR CIRCUS: *(reaching his wits in)* Why won't you just fight me?!

John just looks up at Doctor Circus. It is apparent that John no longer wishes to be any fun whatsoever; he is done playing games.

DOCTOR CIRCUS: Don't you want the fucking world? *(John just stares at him)* Don't you want answers?

John says nothing. Doctor Circus leans in closer.

DOCTOR CIRCUS: Don't you want my hat?

John just sort of scoffs at this, the fucking peasant.

DOCTOR CIRCUS: You're really going to make me do this, aren't you?

Doctor Circus pulls out his knife and goes to Jane 2. She screams as he pulls her up to a kneeling position. He then crouches by her, covering her mouth. He puts the dagger to her throat.

DOCTOR CIRCUS: Are you watching, John?

Doctor Circus goes to slit her throat. Jane 2 screams a shrill scream through his fingers.

JOHN: *(before he slits)* I'll fight you, okay?!

Doctor Circus smirks and stands. He lets the wounded Jane 2 fall to the stage.

DOCTOR CIRCUS: *(having fun)* I'm sorry, what was that?

JOHN: Isn't asking once, enough?

DOCTOR CIRCUS: I suppose we shall see, won't we?

Doctor Circus walks over to John, his knife still drawn. He, for a moment, thinks about cutting John free. He holds back for a second, however, but then he stops before he does anything. He gingerly places his hand on John's shoulder.

DOCTOR CIRCUS: *(seeking clarification)* You are actually going to fight me, aren't you?

JOHN: Why wouldn't I?

DOCTOR CIRCUS: You aren't going to try and escape?

JOHN: Wouldn't that be pointless?

DOCTOR CIRCUS: Do you believe it to be?

JOHN: Do you think I would say so if I didn't believe it to be true?

Doctor Circus eyes John closely. He sizes him up (as the kids would say). He reads John as best he can.

Beat.

Doctor Circus smirks and claps his hands.

DOCTOR CIRCUS: Let's duel, shall we?

Doctor Circus cuts John loose and then walks over to some boxes on the other side of the stage. John rubs his wrists and begins to untie his own legs. Doctor Circus riffles through the box he chose, going through ASSORTED WEAPONRY. As he does this, John is able to untie himself completely.

DOCTOR CIRCUS: Have you had the pleasure of dueling before?

JOHN: *(standing)* Do I seem like the kind of guy who has dueled before?

DOCTOR CIRCUS: Would you be offended if I said "no"?

JOHN: Do you really care if you've offended me?

Doctor Circus walks over toward John and places the weapons on the floor between them.

DOCTOR CIRCUS: Do I seem so crass as to be devoid of all human manners?

JOHN: *(Doctor-Circus-esque)* Would you be offended if I said yes?

DOCTOR CIRCUS: *(laughing/amused)* When did you become so quick?

JOHN: You think I learned it from you?

DOCTOR CIRCUS: Wouldn't that be wonderful if it were true?

JOHN: *(learning sarcasm, all of a sudden)* What's your definition of wonderful?

Doctor Circus stares at John after he says this uncharacteristic quip. It would appear Doctor Circus's amusement has ceased. Perhaps it has. Perhaps he is acting. John doesn't waver either way, though, instead he just meets Doctor Circus's gaze and keeps it. It would appear as though this makes Doctor Circus inquisitive.

DOCTOR CIRCUS: Why don't you just pick your weapon?

JOHN: Don't <u>you</u> have a preference?

DOCTOR CIRCUS: You don't think I'm proficient in all of these things?

JOHN: *(uncharacteristically confident)* So you don't have a specialty?

DOCTOR CIRCUS: *(unenthused)* Will you just pick your weapon?

JOHN: What's the hurry, <u>Mister</u> Doctor Circus?

DOCTOR CIRCUS: Why do you seem so hesitant?

JOHN: Do I seem hesitant to you?

DOCTOR CIRCUS: Yes, are you scared?

JOHN: *(oddly full of fervor)* You want to see scared?!

As quick as John can move, he grabs a SWORD from the pile and charges Doctor Circus. Doctor Circus blocks the blow with his cane, however.

DOCTOR CIRCUS: So you want a dirty fight, huh?

John doesn't answer; he just lunges at Doctor Circus with the sword again. Doctor Circus dodges it, swiftly, and canes John in the leg with a large crack. John cries out in pain and falls to one knee.

DOCTOR CIRCUS: Should I finish you now, John?

JOHN: Do it, why don't you?

DOCTOR CIRCUS: *(laughing)* Where would be the fun in that?

Doctor Circus saunters over to the pile of weaponry and begins to peruse the goods as though he were picking fruit at the local grocer's.

DOCTOR CIRCUS: *(condescending, as always)* Well what have we here?

Doctor Circus bends down to the various weaponry and picks a MACHETE.

DOCTOR CIRCUS: *(looking at the machete)* Is this a machete? It seems a bit small, no?

He shrugs at John's lack of an answer and tosses the machete back down. He then picks up a SICKLE.

DOCTOR CIRCUS: You think this one will be fun, John?

John doesn't answer.

DOCTOR CIRCUS: Huh? Don't you think? *(he eyes the sickle)* But then again, when was the last time I used a sickle?

With that he throws the sickle back into the pile and looks over the pile again.

DOCTOR CIRCUS: Who would've thought this would be so difficult?

He looks to John for something, but John doesn't give him a thing. He laughs at John's silence before he goes back to the weapons. He picks up a PISTOL.

DOCTOR CIRCUS: Could this be the way to go?

John looks away at this; an obvious tell that Doctor Circus notices.

DOCTOR CIRCUS: What do you think, my boy? Seems quick and painless, don't you think? Would that be something you would prefer?

He cocks the gun and points it at John. John tries to stand and run, but he can't. He shields himself in a futile effort.

DOCTOR CIRCUS: *(amused, again)* Really, John? You think I'd keep this thing loaded?

He nonchalantly points the gun toward the audience and it GOES OFF, startling everyone on stage.

DOCTOR CIRCUS: Well how about that then?

He laughs and looks at John, who he expects to have amusement. John has none, however. Instead he just stares daggers at Doctor Circus.

DOCTOR CIRCUS: Well aren't we a little touchy?

He laughs at John before he throws the pistol back into the pile (it doesn't go off, that would be a silly joke to make in such a serious moment). He peruses the weapons again; bending down, and touching each one. His eyes then land on a MACE. It is rather large.

DOCTOR CIRCUS: *(excited)* Oooh, haven't you always wanted to use a mace, John? *(he picks it up and gets a feel for it)* Do you think I could do some damage with it? Do you think you would die when it cracks into your skull, or would you survive and then be forced to struggle through the rest of your life as I turned your body into a nice, pulpy substance with this wonderful weapon of mine?

He waits for John to answer, but again, John doesn't answer.

DOCTOR CIRCUS: Doesn't that just sound like a wonderful time?

Doctor Circus laughs uproariously and then charges John, with a mace above his head. John rolls out of the way as Doctor Circus brings the mace down with a large thud (this should prove that the mace is no real prop).

DOCTOR CIRCUS: When did you become so quick?

John doesn't respond to this, he just hops up, half limping, half jumping on one leg like some sort of buffoon (this will prove to be funny to the most idiotic of audiences, those laughs should be ignored). John is ready to defend himself.

DOCTOR CIRCUS: So cat's got your tongue?

Doctor Circus charges again, John ducks and shoulder checks the mace-wielding master below his knees. Doctor Circus tumbles over John but rolls up in a manner that is very quick.

DOCTOR CIRCUS: *(laughing)* How in the world could I have forgotten that we were fighting dirty? *(calling off)* Will someone cut the lights, please?

The lights are cut and all is dark.

JOHN: What are you doing?

Doctor Circus gives no answer, save for a laugh.

JOHN: Why do you insist on toying with us so?

In the dark, Doctor Circus creeps up to Jane 2 laughing. He touches her and when he does, she screams.

JOHN: Jane? *(there is no response)* What are you doing to her, you bastard?

Doctor Circus produces more laughter as he drags Jane 2 passed John and towards the apron.

JOHN: *(desperate)* Why aren't you answering me?! Huh?! Why?!

Doctor Circus attempts to abscond with Jane 2 through the audience, by dragging her off of the apron. He has a little trouble with this, however, for he can't see all that well in the dark. He can't seem to get her off the stage. It is almost as though she is tethered there. John cannot see what is transpiring.

JOHN: Why do you have to do this every time? *(no response)* Why do you always have to take them? *(no response)* Is it because you need to keep me down? You know I'd defeat you if you didn't fight so dirty? Is that what it is? Is it because you're a fucking coward?

Doctor Circus stops trying to drag her off, struck with a wound to his pride, and hops back on stage.

DOCTOR CIRCUS: What was that you said, Johnny-Boy?

JOHN: Oh, can you not hear? Or did I just hit the nail on the head?

DOCTOR CIRCUS: *(laughing)* When did you become such a feisty cunt?

JOHN: Do you really think name-calling will work?

DOCTOR CIRCUS: Hasn't it before?

John is too frustrated to respond, he just lets out a sigh. He has had enough of this, for the fight in him has dissipated. Doctor Circus laughs at this like a little schoolboy. He then makes his way back OS, behind John.

DOCTOR CIRCUS: Aw, John, what's the matter? Are we not having fun anymore?

JOHN: Has this ever really been fun? Even for you?

DOCTOR CIRCUS: Where have all these questions come from, John? What has come over you?

JOHN: *(laughing)* Did you ever think about what all of this was doing to me? Did you?

DOCTOR CIRCUS: Why, whatever do you mean?

JOHN: Do you realize what it's like to put on the show for you? To lose your wives at your whim?

DOCTOR CIRCUS: Would it help if I told you I was raised by wolves?

JOHN: Is that really even a valid excuse?

DOCTOR CIRCUS: Isn't it better than saying I just don't care?

JOHN: There is no winning with you, is there?

DOCTOR CIRCUS: Has there ever been? *(shouting off)* Are the lights really off?

MINIMAL LIGHTING comes on, it's not enough for a clear view, but enough to see that Doctor Circus has apparently left the stage. John sighs. It can be seen that Jane 2 is lying in the position of the original Jane from ACT I.

JOHN: Won't you just fight me fair and square? Once and for all? Why don't you just turn the lights on in full?

DOCTOR CIRCUS: *(still on stage)* Can you ask nicely?

JOHN: *(sighing)* Will you turn the lights on, <u>please</u>?

Absolutely nothing happens. John just looks around trying to see in the minimal lighting.

JOHN: *(to everywhere)* Hello?

Just then, the lights turn on in full. Doctor Circus jumps on top of the boxes behind John, mace held high above his head. He lets out a primal scream. John turns just as Doctor Circus jumps from the boxes and onto him. Doctor Circus gets stabbed with John's sword in the most stage-fake way; John's sword is held under Doctor Circus's armpit. Despite how fake it all is, Doctor Circus still acts as though he's really been stabbed in a very convincing manner.

DOCTOR CIRCUS: Oh god, why?! Why have I been forsaken?

John steps back as Doctor Circus flails around, dropping his mace on the stage.

DOCTOR CIRCUS: Is this truly the way that I am to go?

Doctor Circus then falls down, weak from imagined blood loss. He crawls towards John and looks up at him.

DOCTOR CIRCUS: *(near death)* Are you proud of yourself, my boy?

JOHN: *(angry)* How many times do I have to tell you that I am not your boy?

DOCTOR CIRCUS: *(looking at John as though what John has just said has wounded him more than his actual "wound")* Et tu, Brute? *(clutching his "wound")* Et tu?

With this, Doctor Circus falls to the stage and "dies". It's fairly obvious that he is faking it, but John believes it. John turns to Jane 2, but then gets wary and realizes he shouldn't turn away from Doctor Circus completely.

JOHN: *(to Jane 2, but looking at Doctor Circus)* Can you believe it Jane? Can you believe I finally got him? We should probably leave before he comes back though, yeah?

Jane 2 doesn't answer. This causes John to turn towards her.

JOHN: Jane, are you okay?

Jane 2 does not answer. She seems nonresponsive, as though her wounds have finally overtaken her.

JOHN: Jane? Jane?!

Again, no answer is provided by Jane 2. This causes John to forget about Doctor Circus and limp over to Jane 2 so he can hold her in his arms.

JOHN: Jane? Are you okay? Can you wake up please? Jane?

The curtains begin to close behind them. The STAGEHANDS pull out the CAR FRONT, complete with the BRANCH this time, and FAKE TREES.

JOHN: Jane? Jane?

The curtains have now closed completely.

END ACT III

ACT IV

The scene is set exactly as it was at the beginning of ACT I. John and Jane 2 are continuing seamlessly from ACT III's end. Smoke begins to creep from the CAR HOOD. Jane 2 and John are still wounded from the previous Act.

JOHN: *(worried)* Jane? Jane?! Oh my god, Jane, please wake up.

Jane 2 stirs and looks at John.

JANE 2: Oh, John, is it really you?

JOHN: Yes, my dear. Are you okay?

JANE 2: Yes, I just had the most horrendous dream. We were held capt- *(she realizes something)* Wait. Have we been in an accident?

JOHN: Yes. I swerved to miss a deer and ran straight into that tree over there.

JANE 2: Oh my, that is awful. Are you okay?

JOHN: Yes, I've just hurt my leg is all. I should be fine though. How are you?

JANE 2: I'm okay. Just a little creeped out from that dream I had. *(looking around/shuddering)* Are you okay to walk? This forest is giving me the willies.

JOHN: I don't think I can walk right now. Maybe someone will come by. Surely this dirt road mustn't be a bust one. Why don't you tell me about your dream?

JANE 2: *(shudders)* No more questions, please.

JOHN: I'm sorry, I just want to know about your dream.

JANE 2: No, I'm sorry. It's just part of the dream. It's all fading around now, though. We were in an accident, like this, and we had to take refuge with a madma-

JOHN: *(notices the blood on Jane 2's costume)* My god.

JANE 2: What?

JOHN: You're bleeding.

JANE 2: What? *(she looks at her hand, which has blood on it)* Oh my god, that looks like a lot of blood.

JOHN: It is. *(thinks about it)* Damnit. *(he gets up, but the pain from his leg shoots up his body)* Ah, damn it all!

JANE 2: Are you okay?

JOHN: Yeah, it's just my leg. I hurt it in the accident. Do you think you can walk?

John tries to steady himself, but the pain is getting the best of him. He hunches over so as to not pass out.

JANE 2: Oh John, I'm worried about you.

JOHN: Don't be, I'll be okay.

JANE 2: I'm also really scared. I don't want to-

JOHN: Shhh, don't say that. I'm scared too, okay?

Just as scared as scared can be, but everything will work out okay, alright? This is just a little mishap.

JANE 2: You promise?

JOHN: With all my heart.

He walks over to her, painfully, and sits next to her. He plays with her hair, sweetly.

Beat.

JANE 2: Did you miss the deer?

JOHN: What?

JANE 2: The deer. Did you miss the deer you swerved to miss? Before you hit the tree?

JOHN: Oh, no, unfortunately not. I clipped him, I'm sure. He was a big buck, though. I'm sure he'll be alright. I still feel awful about the whole thing, though.

JANE 2: Poor deer.

JOHN: I'll be alright.

JANE 2: Not you, dear; the deer, dear.

They chuckle at this. As they do, a faint and ominous humming can be heard coming from OS. It is not audible to the couple immediately.

JANE 2: You know how much I-

JOHN: *(noticing the humming)* Do you hear that?

JANE 2: Hear what?

JOHN: *(whisper)* Listen.

They sit there and listen. The humming gets louder and louder and louder as though it is getting closer.

JANE 2: *(hearing the hum)* Oh my, what is that?

JOHN: I have no idea.

JANE 2: I don't like it, John. It is weirding me out.

JOHN: I'm sure it's nothing.

Just then Doctor Circus comes on to the stage. He is clearly wearing Woe's jester cap underneath his own, all-important hat. He still has his cane, but in his non-cane-holding hand he has a BROOMSTICK WITH GLEE'S JESTER HAT ATOP IT. He looks odd. That is to say, odder than usual. As soon as John and Jane 2 see him, they stand defensively. Jane 2 has less trouble doing so than John. Despite his pain, John still pulls Jane 2 behind him, instinctively, as though he is trying to shield her from something horrid. Jane 2, however, doesn't seem to want protection and so she moves back around in front of John as they look at Doctor Circus. Doctor Circus looks back at them.

DOCTOR CIRCUS: *(as Glee/moving the broomstick with each word/falsetto)* Now, brother, who is that over there I see. *(as Woe/from his own self/vocal fry)* Oh sister, I do not know why you bother asking me.

Doctor Circus and the broomstick Glee share a moment and look at John and Jane 2. He and the stick size them up (as the kids say) and read them like the children's book that they are.

DOCTOR CIRCUS: *(as Woe)* It appears as though they are lost in their travels. *(as Glee)* Are they aware of their fate, which is about to unravel? *(as Woe)* I doubt it, dear sister, however could they know? *(as Glee)* A point, so good, my brother, to them we must go.

Doctor Circus tries his best to laugh as two people. He then creeps over, cautiously towards John and Jane 2 who seem very, very uncomfortable. He circles around them, sniffing them a little bit so as to get a better idea of their scent. Once he's got it, he stands at attention in front of the couple and waves to them.

DOCTOR CIRCUS: *(as Glee)* Hello, fine strangers. How do you do? *(as Woe)* I am Woe; *(moves the broomstick up and down)* this is Glee, 'tis nice to meet you.

John and Jane 2 look at each other, a little afraid. Doctor Circus clears his throat and this causes John to snap back into reality.

JOHN: Oh, um, hi. I'm John and look, we need some help real bad. I think I'm quite hurt and my wife here seems to be bleeding a lot. Is there any way you could help us?

DOCTOR CIRCUS: *(as Woe)* Why sure, my good man, whatever you need. *(as Glee)* We'll do what we can, no matter the deed.

JOHN: Well, do you have a car?

DOCTOR CIRCUS: *(as Glee)* Well no, in that way, we cannot assist. *(as Woe)* There is another option, if you will enlist.

JOHN: What option is that?

DOCTOR CIRCUS: *(as Woe)* Just follow us to the mansion on high. *(as Glee)* There you will meet one special guy. *(as Woe)* He will help you with everything in the reach of his hands. *(as Glee)* He is the upmost respectable, the gentlest man.

JOHN: Does he have a phone?

DOCTOR CIRCUS: *(as Glee)* I assure you, this man has any desire. *(as Woe)* And if he does not, you may call her a liar.

JOHN: Well... *(turns to Jane 2)* What do you think?

Jane 2 looks as though she is about to faint. Her wounds might be trying to overtake her again.

JOHN: Are you okay Jane?

Jane 2 doesn't answer.

JOHN: *(nudging Jane 2)* Jane?

JANE 2: *(shoots awake)* Huh?

JOHN: Jane, are you okay?

JANE 2: *(weakly)* I'm fading fast, John...

JOHN: Oh no! *(to Doctor Circus)* Can we make it to this place you're talking about quickly?

DOCTOR CIRCUS: *(as Woe/to Glee)* Oh joy, the master will be pleased. *(as Glee/to Woe)* Yes, a little company is just what he-

JOHN: *(dire)* Please! We need to hurry! I think she is dying!

DOCTOR CIRCUS: *(as himself)* Alright, alright, jeez. *(back as Glee)* This way, <u>please</u>.

He turns to lead them and the curtains open revealing the full forest and the cardboard cutout of the mansion. They begin to walk towards it.

JOHN: Oh good, is that the mansion?

DOCTOR CIRCUS: *(trying to be both Glee & Woe)* Yes.

JANE 2: *(weakly)* Thank god, I don't know how much longer I can last.

JOHN: *(whisper)* Shhh, everything will be alright soon.

JANE 2: *(whisper)* You promise?

JOHN: *(whisper)* With all my heart.

DOCTOR CIRCUS: *(stopping short/as Glee)* Mouths that whisper should stay shut. *(as Woe)* And throats that murmur deserve to be cut.

JOHN: She just really needs help.

DOCTOR CIRCUS: Ugh, fine, come on.

He stomps off USL. John and Jane 2 look at each other and smile. As they do the STAGEHANDS come out and dress the set in THE HOUSE OF BOXES INTERIOR from SR. Once they are done they exit the stage.

Beat.

Doctor Circus as Glee and Woe enters from SR. The couple follows him. He presents the empty seat that he sat on in ACT I to the couple.

DOCTOR CIRCUS: *(as Woe)* Even though you both are worthless. *(as Glee)* I present to you, Doctor Circus!

He tosses the broomstick and loses the jester hat. He then sits down, quickly, and stands back as though he has just been introduced.

DOCTOR CIRCUS: Hello! Hello! Welcome! How are you doing today? *(notices the blood)* Oh my word, are you alright my dear?

JOHN: No, she's been injured ba-

DOCTOR CIRCUS: WAS I TALKING TO YOU?!

JOHN: I-

JANE 2: Help me, please.

Jane 2 falls over into a heap on the floor.

JOHN: Jane! No!

DOCTOR CIRCUS: Oh god damnit.

JOHN: You have to help her, Doctor Circus.

DOCTOR CIRCUS: What's the fucking point?

JOHN: Wha- How- How can you be so cruel?

DOCTOR CIRCUS: Me? Cruel? Are you serious? After all of this? AFTER EVERYTHING I'VE DONE?! YOU INSOLENT FOOL!

Doctor Circus slaps John across the face. John cowers back.

JOHN: Just please help my wife.

DOCTOR CIRCUS: There is no fucking point!

JOHN: How can you say that?

DOCTOR CIRCUS: Because it is true! She was the last Jane we had, John. The play's over. We're done.

JOHN: The play? What are you talking about?

DOCTOR CIRCUS: Oh so now the serum kicks in.

JOHN: The serum? What? What are you talking about? Won't you just help my wife? Please? I'm begging you.

DOCTOR CIRCUS: John, I'm serious: If you don't knock this pathetic husband routine off, I swear to god I WILL GUT YOU LIKE A FUCKING FISH.

JOHN: I need my wife to live.

DOCTOR CIRCUS: *(giving up)* My fucking god.

Quicker than quick, Doctor Circus produces his dagger and thrusts it into John. John cries out in pain, and it is apparent that the effects of the drug he was slipped earlier wears off instantaneously. He looks down at the knife like he's awoken from a dream.

JOHN: *(can't quite comprehend what is happening)* What the- *(looking up to Doctor Circus)* I <u>loved</u> you more than anything.

Doctor Circus snarls at the word. John starts to laugh. The laughter quickly turns manic and he begins to cackle like he's lost his goddamn mind.

DOCTOR CIRCUS: You ungrateful cunt!

Doctor Circus begins to stab John wildly. John keeps laughing all the while, even as he coughs up blood, until he dies. Doctor Circus looks down at John as he wipes off his dagger on his pants.

DOCTOR CIRCUS: *(shaking his head)* You could have been something, you know that? *(he spits on John's corpse)* Good riddance. *(he moves over to Jane 2)* And you...

JANE 2: *(dying)* Please don't kill me.

DOCTOR CIRCUS: Oh, still alive are we? Well let's take care of that.

He straddles her and grips the dagger fiercely.

JANE 2: Oh god no! No! No! No! No!

DOCTOR CIRCUS: *(beyond angry)* YOU SHUT YOUR FACE FOR ONCE IN YOUR LIFE! *(each word hereafter will be punctuated with a stab)* THIS. IS. ALL. YOUR. FUCKING. FAULT. YOU. MISERABLE. WRETCHED. DUMB. VILE. OBTUSE. FECKLESS. CONNIVING. SULTRY. GOD. KNOWS. WHAT. ELSE. PIECE. OF. SHIT. HARLOT. TAKE. MY. BOY. HUH?

Doctor Circus stops stabbing, throwing the knife away. Jane 2 is very much dead now, but this doesn't stop Doctor Circus from grabbing her face and pulling it close to his.

DOCTOR CIRCUS: I GUESS YOU WIN, HUH? I GUESS YOU FUCKING WIN!

He stands up and looks down at her dead body.

DOCTOR CIRCUS: I guess you win.

He turns away from her and shakes his head.

DOCTOR CIRCUS: *(almost quiet)* I guess you win...

He sighs to himself and then notices someone OSR.

DOCTOR CIRCUS: What the fuck are you looking at?

With that he charges off SR. The sound of slaughter ensues.

DOCTOR CIRCUS; *(OS/recognizing someone)* Oh you! Come here right fucking now!

It sounds as though there is utter calamity back stage. There is screaming and yelling and the sound of throats being slit.

DOCTOR CIRCUS: *(OS)* Why are you running? Huh? Why?

A STAGEHAND runs from SL, followed closely by Doctor Circus. The stagehand trips at about the middle of the stage and Doctor Circus jumps atop him. Doctor Circus kills the stagehand swiftly and cleanly. As soon as this happens ANOTHER STAGEHAND rushes out, attempting to attack Doctor Circus.

Doctor Circus sees it coming from a mile away. The stagehand meets the same fate as the other stagehands before him, except Doctor Circus takes his time with this one. Once he's done, he stands up and looks around.

DOCTOR CIRCUS: Is there anyone else? *(he looks SR)* Anyone? *(looks SL)* Hello?

He walks the length of the stage downwards, peeking within the wings as though he is playing hide and seek. He's looking for anything to catch his eye. Something does.

DOCTOR CIRCUS: *(heading towards the wings)* Ah-ha! You! Come here!

He runs fully OS.

VOICE OF A STAGEHAND: *(OS)* No! No! No, please! NOOOOOOOOOOOOOOOOOOOOOOOOOO!

Slicing and dicing can be heard and then all is quiet.

Beat.

Doctor Circus then trudges out, he looks as though he is exhausted. He goes to one of the boxes and opens it up. Inside is the chair from RANT I and BOTTLES OF BOOZE. He sets up the chair and takes out a BOTTLE OF WHISKEY. He opens the bottle and takes a large swig as he drags the chair CS. He keeps drinking and drinking until the bottle is gone.

END ACT IV

RANT IV

Once Doctor Circus has finished the contents of the bottle, he hurls it over his shoulder. He looks around absentmindedly before he sits in the chair. He sulks.

Beat.

Beat.

Beat.

DOCTOR CIRCUS: Is it only me that has ever noticed that silence is unobtainable? No matter how quiet one tries to make it, no matter how silently one tries to live, there will always be noise coming from somewhere. Whether it's a neighbor or a bird or bug. Perhaps it would even be quiet enough for you to hear your own beating heart. Pumping away. Pulsing blood in and out of it so that the world can continue to spin madly on and-

He cuts himself off as he looks out into the audience.

DOCTOR CIRCUS: All I did was dream.

He shakes his head and sits there with his head in his hands.

Beat.

DOCTOR CIRCUS: What use, my friends, is a dream if not to rub it in your face what should be... What could be... *(sighs)* Damn it all. *(he sits back in his chair looking uncomfortable)* I'm done. *(he stands)* I'm done. The play is over, you can all go now.

And with that he hops off the stage and walks down the aisle towards

the back. On the way he huff and puffs, swearing at the attendees and ripping programs from their hands. Finally he makes it to the exit and leaves the stage and theatre.

Beat.

Beat.

Beat.

The lights shoot on. There will be no announcements. There will be no curtain call. There will be no final bow. The audience can go as they please.

END RANT IV

END HOUSE OF BOXES

A NOTE

This note is primarily for the actor who has chosen to undertake the role of Doctor Circus and the director (assuming they are not the same person), but all of those participating in the play may read it if they wish.

It is a time for truth and a time for honesty. You are worthless. You are nothing. You are beyond nothing. You are a black hole of talent and you are lucky to be here. So, I insist, don't forget how lucky you are.

If I had not written this play, then you would have nothing. If I had not conceived of the dialogue, then you would have no words to speak. If I had not scribed the stage directions, then you would have no idea what is happening or what to do. Don't forget that. Don't ever forget that.

What you should do, to show your appreciation, is strike your name from the record. In all programs and promotional material Doctor Circus should be played by "Himself" (assuming you can embody such a god among men) and the play should be directed by Doctor Circus. I know it is a lot to ask, for a man to drop his hubris and give over the credit he never deserved to the man who created it all, but I feel that it must be done. I understand this business is built on taking credit for other's achievements (or at the very least, piggybacking on the more talented), but this master work that I have created deserves to not conform to the normal way the theatre business handles such great works.

So please, remove your name. You are not worthy and you do not deserve it. You know this. I know this. The world doesn't know it yet, but it will. Spare yourself the heartbreak and the embarrassment and succumb to the wishes of the genius author who knows more about everything than you do.

Or, you could be a pathetic, little weasel, who insists on taking the credit. If you are, know this: I would haunt you if you weren't already haunted by the lack of respect you receive from your family, friends, and acquaintances. I hope you rot in hell.

117

<u>COSTUMES</u>

DOCTOR CIRCUS

Top Hat - must be absolutely perfect in everyway
Tailcoat - must be made of the finest materials
Knee Breeches - must be made of the finest materials
Dress Shirt - nice
Socks - long, wonderful socks, that go above the knee
Shoes - like all good shoes, they have buckles
(The clothes will get bloody throughout the performance and should not be washed.)

PERSON FROM THE AUDIENCE

(This person wears whatever people are wearing nowadays. Bell Bottoms? Acid Washed Something? Whatever it happens to be. It would work better if you used an actual person from the audience, but laws are laws I suppose.)

GLEE, THE WOEFUL

Jester's Outfit - a blue-and-silver affair with lots of bells and whistles

WOE, THE GLEEFUL

Jester's Outfit - identical to Glee's except that it is red-and-gold.

ACTOR PLAYING "JOHN"

Shirt - a nice button-up shirt
Tie - a tie that doesn't quite fit right
Slacks - plain-colored pants
Shoes - cheap shoes that were made to look nice
Undershirt - I believe they call them "wife-beaters"
(It can all look a little wrinkled, as though the date he wore the outfit for happened long ago)

ACTOR PLAYING "JANE" 1

Dress - it is something that would be considered "nice" to a plain, sheltered, churchgoer.

Sweater - a plain sweater she uses to cover her shoulders.

Shoes - Mary Janes

Socks - yes, she wears white socks with them, it was her choice not mine.

Hair - her hair should be up in a ponytail

ACTOR PLAYING "JANE" 2

Dress - the same as Jane 1's except this one fits Jane 2 better and even looks better on her, as well.

Sweater - the sweater seems similar to Jane 1's but doesn't look as plain on Jane 2's shoulders.

Shoes - kitten heels, Mary Jane style.

Socks - none

Hair - her hair should be up in a ponytail, but she can take it down at any point after her first appearance if she so wishes.

STAGEHANDS

(It is not the job of the writer to know what the help is wearing, suffice it to say, they should wear what ever they normally wear.)

PROPS

CHAIR - An expensive chair that Doctor Circus adores.

CANE 1 - Doctor Circus's trusty cane. It has an ornate head.

CANE 2 (if necessary) - A replacement for CANE 1, in case it is damaged.

DAGGER - A wonderfully wicked blade that has been sharpened just-so.

TREE PROPS - Numerous cardboard cutouts of trees.

CAR FRONT - The front of a Studebaker 2-door sedan from 1951.

TREE BRANCH - A branch from a tree.

A CARDBOARD CUTOUT OF A LAVISH MANSION - A perfectly rendered recreation of The House of Boxes in flat-cardboard form.

MANTEL - A mantel, the only purpose of which, is to hold up the portrait.

PORTRAIT OF DOCTOR CIRCUS - A portrait of Doctor Circus the person, not the actor playing him.

BOXES - Large, rectangular boxes, that are painted (crudely) many different colors and are filled with many different things.

SOUND BOX - An old sound box, that does have function.

PLATES - The most expensive plates

FORKS - The most expensive forks

KNIVES - Cheap knives.

BUNYIP (cooked) - It must look delicious. [If Bunyip is out of season or unavailable, remember that an average seal can suffice if it is prepared properly].

WINE GLASSES - Plastic wine glasses.

BOTTLE OF WINE - A good vintage of a petite syrah pairs well with Bunyip.

COTS - Specially made cots, that have been fashioned from boxes.

SCRIPT - A copy of either House of Boxes: A Play in Four Acts or another, better play (which you will never find).

AXE - A run of the mill axe.

ASSORTED BOTTLES OF BOOZE - Lots of different types of booze:

    WHISKEY - This is Doctor Circus's favorite and is a

must have in the ASSORTED BOTTLES OF BOOZE.

A POWDERED SERUM - They say it is impossible, but they are wrong.

BROWN BOTTLE - It is small and filled with brown liquid.

SYRINGE - An old syringe that looks as though it has many uses.

POTATOES - Assorted potatoes of different sizes and colors and varieties. No yams.

OLD HARDCOVER BOOKS - Several books. Including (but not limited to): The Bible, Pride & Prejudice, Little Women, Jane Eyre, Wuthering Heights, Anne of Green Gables, Rebecca, The Scarlet Pimpernel, The Scarlet Letter, O, Pioneers!, The Song of The Lark, The Gift of the Magi, North and South, Wives and Daughters, Vanity Fair, The Prisoner of Zenda, Old Yeller, The Call of the Wild, White Fang, Johnny Tremain, Gulliver's Travels, Robinson Crusoe, Swiss Family Robinson, Treasure Island, Around the World in Eighty Days, Twenty-Thousand Leagues Under the Sea, The Jungle Book, The Count of Monte Cristo, Moby-Dick, Don Quixote de la Mancha, The Odyssey, The Brothers Karamazov, Frankenstein, Dracula, The Last of the Mohicans, Dr. Jekyll and Mr. Hyde, The Adventures of Tom Sawyer, The Three Musketeers, Oliver Twist, A Tale of Two Cities, Silas Marner, The Jungle, Ivanhoe, Faust (Parts 1&2), A Doll's House, Les Meserables, Tartuffe or; The Imposter, The Imaginary Invalid, The Seagull, Anna Karenina, War & Peace, One Day in the Life of Ivan Denisovich, Crime and Punishment, The Canterbury Tales, The Aeneid, The Divine Comedy - Paradiso, Purgatoria, & Inferno, *All's Well that Ends Well, As You Like It, The Comedy of Errors, Cymeline, Love's Labours Lost, Measure for Measure, The Merry Wives of Windsor, The Merchant of Venice, A Midsummer Night's Dream, Much Ado About Nothing, Pericles, Prince of Tyre, The Taming of the Shrew, The Tempest, Troilus and Cressida, Twelfth Night, Two Gentlemen of Verona, Winter's Tale, Antony and Cleopatra, Coriolanus, Hamlet, Julius Caesar, King Lear, Macbeth, Othello, Romeo and Juliet, Timon of Athens, Titus Andronicus, Henry IV, Part 1, Henry IV, Part 2, Henry*

*V, Henry VI, Part 1, Henry VI, Part 2, Henry VI, Part 3,
Henry VIII, King John, Richard II, Richard III,* The
Passionate Pilgrim, The Tao Te Ching, The Art of War,
The Wonderful Wizard of Oz, *etc.*

*[It should be noted that all of the Shakespeare should be burned
and badly damaged. His work is atrocious and the people who
wrote under his name are put on too high a pedestal.
Shakespeare's work is only good for kindling and coasters.]*

WOMEN'S LINGERIE - Assorted attractive garments of all
shapes and sizes that must be the epitome of sensual and
seductive.

RANDOM BITS OF MEAT - Beef, lamb, rabbit, pork, elephant,
tiger, dog, etc. [NO CHICKEN]

STUFFED ANIMALS - A variety of stuffed animals that have
been cherished by (and then stolen from) children.

GAS MASKS - Various gas masks from The Great War Era.

BUBBLE WRAP

PACKING PEANUTS

HATCHET - A farmer's hatchet, used to decapitate disgusting
chickens.

PANTRY DISHES - The finest china money can buy.

BALLS OF YARN - A variety of color and style.

EMPTY WATER PITCHER- A pitcher as empty as your mind.

SPORTS BALLS - Different types of sports balls. Must include:

> FOOTBALL - This could be an American Football or a
> proper one, it doesn't really matter in the slightest. Both
> should be in the box, put the prop that is handled can be
> whichever.
>
> BILLIARD BALL - The yellow-striped nine ball.

ASSORTED WEAPONRY - All the types of weapons that can
be imagined need to be represented here. This also
must include:

> SWORD - A fine rapier should do just fine.
>
> MACHETE - Small.
>
> SICKLE - Hand grip.
>
> PISTOL (with blanks) - A beautiful gun, from a more
> elegant age.
>
> MACE - Horrifyingly powerful.

BROOMSTICK GLEE - A broomstick with Glee's jester hat put
atop it.

ACKNOWLEDGMENTS

This book would not be possible without the following people:

Me, Doctor Circus.

That is all.

I know that other people were involved in the making of this play, this version in particular, but their contributions were minimal at best, and nonexistent at worst. Those who were so lucky to be placed in the minimal category mentioned above, were driven to be so great and helpful by me, and me alone. Most of them had very little coursing through their veins until I came along. Take Marc, Miguel, Mikey, and Antonio for instance. The four of them were just aimless wanderers until I gave them purpose. Much like Jeff. Then there's Opal and Omar, two people who desperately needed to give their money away, they only needed me to take it. Or Marion, who felt the need to give input and critiques that fell on deaf ears. And, of course, there's Kurt, Donovan, Leah, Simon, Pedro, and Nicolas. They needed greatness, but could not produce their own, and so they came to me to use mine. Unlike Jessica and Alejandro†, who never needed greatness or wanted it, but they were stuck with it just the same.

Of course, despite the fact I did all of this work myself, I would like to thank the maddening cries of Moira and Aoife who still haunt me to this day. They keep me up at night so that I may work. In the daylight, they stir something inside

---

† For a varying degree of humor, substitute "Jessica and Alejandro" with "Virginia and Benito".

of me, pushing me to darkness, driving me away from the light, bringing me, inevitably, closer to home.

One day I will find you again, and one day this will all stop, but until then, I hunt for you and in doing so I find perfection, a perfection I am able to transcribe into words that are written for peons of varying degrees of brainlessness to perform or even just to read.

There is no end to the genius that I bestow upon the world and so that is why I thank no one, here. Not a single other living soul has had any effect on me what so ever. I was born into this body, into this soul, into this existence that was meant to go down this path that would lead to one undeniable truth: I Am a god.

Not a god in the sense of these new-timey gods, the ones who make promises they cannot follow through on or the one's who demand sacrifice after sacrifice after sacrifice in order for a mortal to be a part of their little divine club. No, I am not like that. I am a god from days of old. I am a god of mischief. I know I am better than all of you and so I will make you my pawns whenever I get bored. It will be fun for me and, if you play your cards right, fun for you as well.

ABOUT THE AUTHOR

Doctor Circus was begat as Doctor Circus, III on December 25th in 1939 by Dr. Doctor Circus, II, and Aibreann **[last name redacted]**. After the murderous demise of his father shortly after his birth, Doctor Circus decided since he was, in fact, the only living Doctor Circus that he should remove the "III" from his name so that he could avoid any confusion with anyone as foolish as to think that maybe he wasn't the *best* Doctor Circus.

After the death of Dr. Doctor Circus II, Aibreann was never seen again, and Doctor Circus was sent out into the world on his own. Strife and many struggles befell the young lad, for he was only a boy, but the Second Great War was transpiring and it made it easy for him to sneak around the world, unnoticed, undetected, all but an invisible blip in the world. He made his way to The Far East and met a fair maiden there. For a brief point in time, he thought about settling down there, building his father's House of Boxes up on a hill somewhere in The Orient and starting a life with this maiden.

Yet, then something quite strange happened. This woman he had met began to change. She began to transform herself into a wicked and twisted, mangled monster that became unrecognizable to Doctor Circus in any way whatsoever. She then began to lash out and attack violently, and unfortunately, there was only one thing to be done. Doctor Circus did what he had to do to survive and he left The Orient for greener pastures.

He then traveled the world, in search of a place to build his home, letting temptations of the mind and body be a thing of the past. He had one goal, and one goal only: He needed to lay roots. He needed to build the House and start the job that was bestowed upon him. At this point, in his story, time was running out and there was much that needed to be done, so he laid the foundation for what would become the extravagant House of Boxes in the first city he could: Tartu.

It was far from ideal, his first House of Boxes, but it would have made Dr. Doctor Circus, II, proud. When that realization struck the current Doctor Circus, he burned the damned thing to the ground and set out of find a new home for the house, settling for idyllic [location redacted], and it is here that things truly became magnificent.

Doctor Circus hired on staff, consisting, primarily, of two clowns who were at his beckon call, and were just so delightful. Their names were [full name redacted] and [full name redacted] and they became rocks on which the foundation of The House of Boxes could be built.

It was a marvelous time, the dawn of The New House, and everything was going, as it should. Except for one thing. Doctor Circus began to feel lonely. Not lonely as it would be felt by you or I, but lonely as in bored. It was a deep, deep boredom and it began to tunnel a void into his very heart.

Luckily for him, unexpected visitors came on a cold October evening and changed everything in Doctor Circus's life for the better. They were Leonard [last name redacted] and [full name redacted], two strangers lost in the night, scared and alone, also injured, if the stories that have been passed down are true. They were seeking shelter and food, and other things that they could not even comprehend they needed. Doctor Circus could not help but take pity on them and they could not help but accept his offer of a place to stay.

They stayed with Doctor Circus for quite sometime before [full name redacted] succumbed to her injuries and left Leonard in a pit of despair, for some reason. With just he and Doctor Circus there in The House of Boxes, by themselves (except for [full name redacted] and [full name redacted], of course), a friendship began to form. To be honest, it was a strange friendship, not so much chum-to-chum, but something more familiar, like brothers or spouses.

Leonard became like a son to Doctor Circus and he started to view Doctor Circus like a father in turn. Rumors began to circulate in **[location redacted]** that this new turn in their relationship was only because of something the locals of the area referred to as *"Norrmalmstorgssyndromet"*. This was not true, however. It was something more than just that. It was something deeper. Something pure. Something that no one else on the planet could ever understand.

Soon, however, their relationship took a turn that neither of them expected nor wanted. You see, Leonard wanted more. The companionship that he and Doctor Circus shared was not enough for him. And this grew a schism between them.

Leonard knew of the schism before Doctor Circus did. It was a schism of that nature; a one-sided kind of void in which one dare not traverse too close to it (for fear of falling in) and the other, the unaware party, was blissfully fine with tumbling into it, head over heels. Ignorance really was bliss.

Yet, like bliss, ignorance must come to an end and one day a conversation happened between the two of them. It was a rainy night and the two of them were in the parlor. **[full name redacted]** and **[full name redacted]** had been sent away for the night, Doctor Circus needed them no longer. Leonard sat near the fire, staring into it, absentmindedly, as though the dancing flames might tell him an answer he desperately was searching for, yet never asked the question to. He didn't even know what the question was. He knew parts of it. He knew it pertained to he and Doctor Circus. Furthermore, he knew it pertained to their relationship, but the intricacies of the question itself escaped him, and, if he were honest, it was driving him mad. Not Doctor-Circus-mad, but mad all the same.

127

Doctor Circus sat in his chair. He watched Leonard for quite some time. He could tell that his friend was struggling with something, and after much internal debate he decided that maybe it was time for them to talk about it. Something was amiss about them. This strange silence they had been living through needed to cease. So he stood, went to the bar, poured himself a drink, drank it and then poured another. He thought about downing it also, but opted to wait. He felt his mind should be clear for the conversation they needed to have.

"Are you doing okay, Leonard?" he asked, walking over to him, so as to be in his eyesight.

"Yes," Leonard said, not looking up from the fire.

"Are you sure, my boy?" Doctor Circus took a sip from his glass, he again thought about finishing it, but he wanted to keep his wits. "You seem as though something is taxing on your conscience."

"I'm not 'your boy'," Leonard said coldly, eyes steady on the flame.

"Excuse me?" Doctor Circus gripped his glass; it made a sound as though it could shatter.

"Sorry," Leonard said, realizing his faux pas, "I don't know what's coming over me recently. Could I get one of those?" He pointed to Doctor Circus's drink.

"Sure," Doctor Circus said, deciding that he should let bygones be bygones.

He then walked over to the bar and poured a drink for Leonard. He finished his own drink and refilled his glass. A large sigh escaped his lips before he picked up both drinks and walked them to Leonard. He handed Leonard his drink and watched as he drank from it.

"So please," Doctor Circus then said, "do tell me what is on your mind, and don't you dare take that tone with me again."

"I won't," Leonard hung his head, "and I want to apologize again. There's just been a lot going on inside my head. It isn't your fault, but I am having these thoughts that I can't escape."

"What are these thoughts, my bo-" Doctor Circus caught himself, "I mean, *Leonard*."

"I don't know," Leonard said as though he's given up, "I just feel so lonely."

"Ha!" Doctor Circus laughed, "How can you feel lonely? Am I not enough? Does our friendship mean nothing? What about **[full name redacted]**? Or **[full name redacted]**, for Christ's sake? Is this house empty? Am I missing something?"

"No, no, it's not that." Leonard took a drink. "Honestly, I just find myself missing **[full name redacted]** recently. She meant a lot to me and you-"

"I told you not to utter her name again!" Doctor Circus shouted, "You know what we re-named her! How dare you act like such a fucking dolt! You know what this means, don't you?"

"No, please…" Leonard pleaded.

"Yes," Doctor Circus, "It is the third rule. If I let you into my home you must obey them. What was the third rule, Leonard?"

"I-I-I don't-"

"You must give me your name," Doctor Circus then said, calmly and coolly as he's ever been. "I need it all."

"No," Leonard said, "I like my name. It was my father's name before me. It means the world to me."

"I am your father now!" Doctor Circus spat, "Don't you see that? I am your father and your mother and your friend and your god! I am your landlord and there are rules you must adhere to and this rule is of third-most importance. I am nothing if not a stickler for the rules."

Leonard went to speak, but there was nothing to say. He knew he had broken the rule. He knew he was wrong. There was nothing he could do. Time worked in a linear fashion for him and he had already moved from Point A, through Point B and now here he was, at Point C. He would have to reap what he had sown.

"What will you call me, then?" He asked Doctor Circus, the tone of surrender hung on his words.

"John," said Doctor Circus, "You shall be John now."

"Okay," John could not have sounded more dejected.

"What is the matter?" Doctor Circus said with a devilish smirk, "Do you not like your new name?"

"Well," John said after some thought, "it is just kind of plain, isn't it?"

"Unbelievably so," Doctor Circus agreed, "but at least it isn't *Ian* or some other horrible name like that."

"True, but still," John said, "I thought we were closer than that."

"I thought so too," Doctor Circus retorted. "I thought so too," he reiterated. "But here we are. You've made your bed, so now you lie in it. That is the way."

"I know," John said as he looked down at his drink, debating whether he should drink from it or not. At this moment he felt unworthy. Doctor Circus could see it on him.

Doctor Circus then felt bad.

"Listen," Doctor Circus then said, "how about we do this…" Before he could finish his thought, though, he realized that his drink was empty.

John watched him as he walked over to the bar and poured a drink. He watched as Doctor Circus drank the first drink, and then poured another. He watched as his re-namer then did it again. And again. And again. Then Doctor Circus walked back over and stood where he was as though nothing had happened.

"What was I saying?" Doctor Circus asked.

"You just said," John began before he quoted, "'Listen, how about we do this…' Then you trailed off and poured yourself a drink."

"Ah, yes," Doctor Circus thought, "so where was I?"

He then looked down and paced for a bit before: "Ah, yes! I was going to tell you about my play."

"Your play?" John asked. "Which play are you talking about?"

"I'm working on a play, my John," Doctor Circus proclaimed proudly, "and I'm going to need you to be in it."

"What is it about?"

"This house!" Doctor Circus exclaimed, "And you and I and **[full name redacted]** and **[full name redacted]**! Everything. All of it. It will be a thing that has never existed. And a thing that will never exist after. I'll write some of it, but most of it will flow free. Then we can keep what sticks. The main character will be me, but there is a character named John that I think you would be perfect for."

"I can't play a John if my name is John," John said. "That would be ridiculous don't you think?" John then clarified, so as not to offend: "Not that I think it's ridiculous, but someone might and if they are a certain someone who might have power, perhaps they won't like the play and it won't go into the annals of history, like it should."

John nearly produced excrement on himself as he watched Doctor Circus ponder the words that had just come out of his mouth. He could see Doctor Circus roll the words around his mind, examining each one, not just for its meaning but for its tone and inflection. He always weighed these things and it always made John's bowels feel as though they may loosen, unexpectedly. But then:

Doctor Circus spoke, "I agree." A sigh of relief emitted from John. "You are right."

Doctor Circus then seemed to ponder this for quite some time. John just watched him.

"So what should we do about this?" Doctor Circus asked, finally.

131

"I don't know," John said, "It's your play. I'm not as smart as you."

"That is true," Doctor Circus said as he thought. "How about we do this: We give you an alias for the play. You can be some other name. We can change it for each performance if need be. It might be nice and refreshing to deal with the stage in such a way."

"I like that," John said with a laugh, "you know I hate the theatre."

"We both do."

"Yes." John concurred, again laughing. "But what should I be called then?"

"How about **[alias redacted]**?" Doctor Circus said without very much thought.

"**[alias redacted]**?" John repeated, letting each syllable roll around in his mind. "Isn't that also pretty plain?"

"Well yes **[alias redacted]** is, but that isn't such a bad thing," Doctor Circus said matter-of-factly, "plainness makes the world go 'round."

"Okay," John said, "I trust you."

"As you should," Doctor Circus said with a smirk. "Now, I am going to go write this play, or at least as much of it as it seems fit."

And with that, Doctor Circus filled up his drink and then left the parlor. John watched after him and went back to staring at the fire, his question still forming in his mind.

John's fragments of a question were of no importance to Doctor Circus. He was on a mission then. He had been planning on writing a play, a masterpiece, for quite some time, but now that he had put it out into the universe, it had to be completed. So with that thought in his mind he retired to his study and did not leave until he had a rough draft of a script.

When he was done he showed it to John, **[full name redacted]**, **[full name redacted]**, and the corpse of [full name redacted], who John didn't know existed still. Doctor Circus felt that he would take it the wrong way (which he did when he found out years and years later).

The reviews were far from mixed. Each of them agreed that it was the best thing they had ever read. More than that, they all agreed, unanimously, that it was the best thing that had ever been conceived.

"It's genius," said John.

"Superb, for this day," said [full name redacted].

"Unmatched, so I say," said [full name redacted].

"This, without any doubt is the most well thought-out, play- neigh, piece of literature -that I have ever read. You are wonderful, Doctor Circus, and this play is everything you embody, in the best possible way," said the corpse of [full name redacted] but not aloud, for that would be crazy.

With such high praise being the wind in his sails, Doctor Circus then staged the first performance of the play in [location redacted], and it received all the acclaim he rightly deserved, and despite the incident (that will hereto be referred to as "The Incident") it was demanded that he continue to perform the show.

And so he did, for years and years. It changed from birth, grew as any good child does, and it really took its stride in adolescence. It's then when, for metaphorical purposes, it reached puberty and when it reached puberty the United States of America came a-callin' and that call was more than answered by Doctor Circus.

This call brought anxiety to Doctor Circus, however, for when America calls and asks something of you, those expectations must be met. So with that in mind, Doctor Circus pulled the play from production so that they could do one thing they had never done: they rehearsed and prepared appropriately.

The rehearsal schedule was strenuous. Various sources report various things. Some say it was six hours a session, the others say it was 24-hours a session, others still report days-upon-days of not stopping the repetition of lines over and over and over and over and over and over again until people fell and actresses were replaced. Regardless of what is to be believed, the time spent trying to fine-tune something that is already perfect proved to be too much for some people, John in particular (if the actresses aren't to be considered).

This is why John felt the need to cause a scene one day.

"We can't take this anymore," said John one day after quite the strenuous rehearsal session, "this is too much Doctor Circus."

"'Too much'?" Doctor Circus said, calmly, "TOO FUCKING MUCH?! DO YOU KNOW WHAT THAT EVEN MEANS? GODDAMNIT, JOHN OR **[alias redacted]** OR WHATEVER-YOUR-NAME-IS, CAN YOU EVEN FATHOM, IN THAT IDIOT BRAIN OF YOUR'S, WHAT THAT EVEN FUCKING MEANS?! 'TOO FUCKING MUCH'?! MY GOD YOU MORONIC PIECE OF SHIT, DO YOU EVEN KNOW OR UNDERSTAND WHAT WE'RE DOING HERE?"

"NO," John retorted, meeting Doctor Circus's calm timbre with his own, "NO I FUCKING DON'T AND NO ONE HERE DOES, FOR THAT MATTER." John was very upset at this point. So upset, in fact, that he approached Doctor Circus, his pointer finger outstretched almost violently. "YOU NEED TO CUT THIS SHIT OUT! ISN'T IT ENOUGH THAT YOU PUT **[full name redacted]** IN THE CRAZY HOUSE AND SENT **[full name redacted]** AND **[full name redacted]** TO THEIR GRAVES? NOT TO MENTION WHAT YOU DID TO **[full name redacted]** AND JUST THINK OF WHAT **[full name redacted]**'S MOTHER MUST THINK! CAN'T YOU SEE WHAT A MONSTER YOU'VE BECOME?" John just stared at

Doctor Circus then. They both breathed heavy. "Can't you see it, Doctor Circus? Can't you see what you are now?"

"I am what I've always been," Doctor Circus answered, "Can't you see that? Can't you see what I am? I've always been this. Honestly, I'm glad you see it now. It's such a relief." Doctor Circus laughed at this like he had made a joke. "But with that relief comes an affront, and affronts can only be met with one thing."

"And what is that?"

"A duel? A fight?" Doctor Circus's signature smirk was brandished across his face, "To the death, of course."

"Why do you always want to fight?" John asked, knowing it would offend Doctor Circus greatly.

"Because it's the only way our fifth act can end!" Doctor Circus shouted this as though it were the most truthful thing he had ever said.

"There are no acts in life!" John shouted this as though it meant something.

"Are you saying that we should move it into the fourth act?" Doctor Circus really wanted to know the answer to this question.

"There is no play, you fucking jackass," John said, and he said it with such fervor and force that it reverberated off all of the walls in their practice space.

A silence then hung in the air, as though it were a thick fog. No one knew what to say. Not the actors or actresses, nor the stagehands. Neither John nor even Doctor Circus. There was just a thick wetness on them. It didn't leave them sopping, but they were all uncomfortable. Every last one of them.

"Fine," Doctor Circus then said, "if that is how you feel, then kill me."

"I wo-"

"KILL ME!" Doctor Circus said as he threw a sword (one that they were using as a prop, that was not an actual prop) to John. "DO IT NOW."

135

"I won't." John said sternly.

"You milquetoast. You twat." Doctor Circus was laughing maniacally now, no one witnessing it felt comfortable in the slightest. "You lack that which is between my legs. You can't even fathom what such a thing would feel like. You are nothing. You are always nothing. You will never be anything other than nothing. You know that and so that is why it is so funny to me that you can't speak up like you thought you could. You are a bitch with no bite. A little dog, worse than a bitch, actually. You are a male dog who has been neutered. You are so far removed from the canine hierarchy that not a Greek letter exists to define what kind of male you are. You are negative. You are nothing. You are a fool and a dolt and a scoundrel and if you ever speak to me this way again I will cut off your tongue and shove it so far up the twat of your mo-"

Before Doctor Circus could finish what he was saying, the blade of a sword was thrust into his gut. While he had been talking, John had grabbed the sword from the floor. He had thought about what he was going to do with it and, while Doctor Circus bloviated on, John came to the conclusion that he should thrust it into Doctor Circus and end the inane droning that was transpiring.

Doctor Circus fell to his knees and looked up at John. There was a strange expression on his face, a queer emotion in his eye. It's something most people could relate to, but when John saw it on Doctor Circus's face it seemed like something foreign. When John realized what it was, a deep darkness settled in his gut.

"I'm so sorry," John said.

"I loved you," Doctor Circus said.

"You can't say that," John retorted.

"I can say what I want in my house."

"This isn't your house anymore."

"It will always be my house." Doctor Circus laughed, and the laughter never left his eyes. It just froze in them, still and pure, as his breath left him and he collapsed on the floor.

John thought it was over then. John thought he had put it all behind him. He felt free and clear and he wept briefly as he looked down at the body of a man he once viewed as his father. Feelings erupted in him at the moment. He missed him, first and foremost, but he also remembered all of the Janes and he knew that what he did was right. For a moment, he started to feel like a hero.

Before that heroicness could overtake him, something spectacular happened:

Doctor Circus rose like a phoenix from death's grasp. What John didn't know- what he could not know -is that Doctor Circus had stared death in the face nearly a million times and he knew how to escape it.

Unfortunately for John, Doctor Circus's reentrance required a sacrifice. That sacrifice needed to be John's existence. And with Doctor Circus's first new breath, John was no more.

This put a chink in that, which was the heavy-metal armor of a play that Doctor Circus had conceived. This chink was easily mended, however, and so Doctor Circus absconded with **[full name redacted]** and **[full name redacted]** to The United States of America, to finally put on the play they had called for.

Unbeknownst to Doctor Circus, however, he had taken too much time trying to perfect his already perfect masterpiece and the opportunity that he had in the U.S.A. had come and gone. Not wanting to let the bastardly bitch of a world get the best of him, he went south to **[location redacted]**, a place he referred to as "the first world's idea of a third world", where he recast his show with an all new cast and crew that were from **[full name redacted]** and the surrounding area.

This was, for all intents and purposes, a complete and utter disaster.

The play *The House of Boxes: Part the First (abridged)*, as it was known then, was non-hyperbolically run out of town (not actually but figuratively, that is to say that they most definitely demanded he leave, but there were no pitchforks involved). From the first night Doctor Circus ran into town, with his ambitions so grandiose (the townspeople of **[location redacted]**'s words, not mine), everyone thought that he was trouble. It was a stigma he could not escape. They thought that what he demanded was too much of the people of **[location redacted]**. But that was not the case. He demanded the world of them, that is to be sure, but he wouldn't have done it without the clear and true thought that they could have given it to him. The people of **[location redacted]** are intelligent people. They could do anything they set their minds to. How could Doctor Circus be perceived as a villain when all he ever thought of the people of **[location redacted]** was that they could accomplish anything? It didn't make sense to him.

I mean, were they **[full name redacted]** or **[full name redacted]**, or even **[full name redacted]**, for that matter? Did they think they could act with **[full name redacted]**'s verbosity or **[full name redacted]**'s nonchalance? Were they held in such high regard as **[full name redacted]** or **[full name redacted]**? Were their opinions as pertinent as **[full name redacted]**'s? Or **[full name redacted]**!? That is to say that **[full name redacted]**'s opinions are considered important and they dictated what other people's opinions are, but then how could **[full name redacted]**'s opinions be as important as **[full name redacted]**'s? It just made no sense. It would be one thing if **[full name redacted]** or Vladimir Putin said it. Their opinions mattered, at least to Doctor Circus, but the point-of-fact was that they didn't sound like them at all. They might as well have been **[full name redacted]** or **[full name redacted]**, for all the good it did.

Yet it didn't matter who said what. All that was important was that the people in **[location redacted]** were boiling before their pot was even put on the stove. They didn't like Doctor Circus. He didn't care, however. He was just trying to put on a show that Doctor Circus would be proud of. It was all about him. It had never been about anybody else. And the people in the first world's idea of a third world needed to know that.

And so he put on a once-nightly performance of the show in various locations throughout **[location redacted]**. He moved around. He made sure that the people who had it out for him couldn't follow him around. The show must go on. And it truly must. Whoever coined the phrase "the show must go on"* had no idea that such a thing as *The House of Boxes: Part the First (abridged)* would ever exist. If they did know that, they would have surely tried to turn this mere phrase into a law that would be passed down from dictator to dictator. At least that is how it would appear that Doctor Circus felt about it. That phrase burrowed inside him and it drove him through every upscale theatre and dive bar in **[location redacted]**.

---

* The phrase appears to originate from an old circus tradition where if an animal escaped or a performer was incapacitated, it was the job of the ringmaster and/or the other performers in the show to keep up a façade of all-is-well so as to insure that the audience would not panic, for it was a point of honor to not leave other performers deserted when there was no replacement (or "understudy", as would come to be the term to use in later understandings of the phrase) available at that juncture. No singular person is credited with coming up with the phrase, and so that is why "whoever" is used in place of the person's actual name.

Unfortunately, at some point, the bad things that bad men had said caught up to him and his show and so he moved it north of the border.

The play didn't fare any better in **[location redacted]**, however. The bad reviews from their neighbor down south had made its way over the **[location redacted]** and passed the **[location redacted]**. The play and Doctor Circus were doomed from the start. That didn't stop him, however and he preformed it all the same.

He watched with pride (while performing in it) as the play ebbed and flowed freely. It moved from city to city, protesters be damned. And within that ebbing or flowing it grew into something more than Doctor Circus ever could have expected. It became what it is today.

Doctor Circus couldn't be prouder of his work. He knows it is read more than it is preformed, now, but that does not stop him from feeling a father's pride when he looks at it. He cherishes it dearly, more than anything, except for himself because he is all things wonderful.

Currently, Doctor Circus and his House of Boxes reside in **[location redacted]**. He lives with **[full name redacted]**, **[full name redacted]** and **[full name redacted]** (his current John) and finds himself content. He is waiting for more, however. Something deeper. Something that will awake his soul from its current state of ennui. He doesn't think it will be another play, or a book even, that would be pedantic. It will be something much bigger than that. Something the world will revel in. It is coming. It is coming soon. You have been warned.

AN INTERVIEW WITH THE AUTHOR

The air is still and calm in the little rental villa Doctor Circus had arranged for the interview when I am let in by his servants. He sits there, on his chair, as one would expect him. He is quiet. That is unexpected. I sit across from him and put on my recorder. I decide I am the one that needs to break the silence.

Hello, Mr. Doctor Circus, before we start I just wanted to say what a fan I am of yours.

Why thank you, you have no idea what that means.

Would you mind if we start the interview?

Not at all. That's why you're here, isn't it?

Yes, so it is. Let's see. So there's one question that seems to be on everyone's mind that has read your play. It's this: What is The House of Boxes made of? I know that there's the little one made of cardboard, does that mean we're supposed to believe the whole thing is made of that?

It's not made of cardboard. It's made of boxes.

Yes, but what are the boxes made of?

Box materials. Wood and metal. Same things that make a house. That's why we've been making houses out of them. We can just pack up and move the whole thing quickly. It's quite easy. Although it's a shame when something you need is in a box that's used in the foundation.

I bet. Speaking of moving, how often would you say you move around? I've heard it happens a lot.

Yes, we have had to move around quite a bit. It is a little annoying, if I'm honest.

Why is that?

Various reasons. Townspeople, bad smells, police inquiries, boredom.

Police inquiries?

I told you we weren't going to discuss those.

Oh, right, sorry. Curiosity.

It killed the cat.

Yes. Indeed. So do you have plans on settling down, then? Or do you think there will be another move in your future?

I don't know. I can't predict the future. I'm here for now and will stay here for as long I see fit. Can I ask you a question now?

Sure.

Can I get you a drink?

Oh... Um yeah. I'll have whatever you're having.

Very good.

At this point in the interview Doctor Circus gets up and walks out of the room. He is gone for quite some time. I can't be sure of the timing of it because I had to surrender my watch at the door and my recorder seemed to glitch out here, skipping from when he last spoke to when I began speaking again as though nothing was missed. He eventually came back after what must have felt like an hour with two glasses of something brown, presumably whiskey. It should be noted that there was something different about Doctor Circus when he came back. I couldn't put my finger on it, but I do feel it is worth pointing out here.

Thank you.

You are welcome. So, shall we get back to this interview?

Yeah, we ca- Are you using an accent now? I mean, have you always had one?

Ha! Of course I have. Perhaps it's the drink that's bringing it out in me.

Where is it from?

Oh, it's just something I've acquired over the years.

I see. Well I guess that's a good segue into my next question. Would you mind telling me where you're from?

Originally or recently?

Originally, if you wouldn't mind.

Well, honestly, I don't know. I was young when I was born and my family moved around a lot. I did just come from The Pacific Northwest, however.

That's interesting. United States?

Canada.

What were some of the places you moved to as a child? Were they all in Europe or did you come to The States before then?

It was Europe mostly. We went through Asia and Africa a few times. We weren't in the same place very often. That's why The House of Boxes isn't truly a burden on me, like it has been to others.

There have been others "in charge" of The House of Boxes before?

Yes.

So it's not your idea, originally?

Nothing is original, my boy.

Well who's idea would you say the play was, then? If you had to track it all the way back.

Mine.

But you just said-

I was talking about The House itself, not the play which is named after it. If you can not keep up with what is being said, perhaps you should move on.

Wait, so are you telling me that The House of Boxes is an actual place?

Yes, my boy, I thought you knew. Didn't you ask me about it earlier? If it was made of cardboard?

I meant the one in the play.

Well the one in the play and the one in reality are made of the same material. One's just make believe, the other is true.

Where is it located?

I can't tell you that.

Why can't you tell me?

Because it's a secret. Secrets must be earned.

How does one go about earning that secret?

Ha! Would you really like to know? Or is it just a passing curiosity?

Passing curiosity, I suppose. This is an interview. I've got to do my job.

Of course you do. And I have to do mine. To know where The House of Boxes is means that you have found it. It's not my job to give you directions.

So are you some sort of groundskeeper? Or a guardian?

Guardian is apt, I suppose. Although I find I might be a guardian from it not for it.

The House of Boxes is dangerous?

Of course, have you not read the play?

Of course I have. I really like the play. But it seems like you- your character -is the danger there.

Really? That's strange. I had always intended for Jane to be the villain. Or at least John. They got afraid. Their fear made them evil.

Do you think that truly comes across in the work?

Yes, it should at least.

What would you say to someone who told you that they didn't get that particular theme?

I'd call them a dolt. Jane's the clear villain. Using her victimhood to sway John to kill. Just because she acts helpless doesn't mean she is. It just means she wants you to think she is. Isn't that worse? Isn't that just wretched? Sure, I can be abrasive. I'm not doubting that. But I only go so far. Those who play the victim for gain tend to be a special kind of wicked. That is why all the Janes are the worst.

All the Janes?

Yes, every last one.

Do you feel as though you have something against all women? Or is it just those women that have the name Jane?

I adore women. I really do. All those that I've named Jane, however, are the absolute worst, vile, women that have ever walked this earth. That much I can assure you. I've never met a man so evil.

So are you saying that men are better than women? In your opinion?

I don't bother myself with those concerns. I'm better than them. Both of them. Men and women alike. They're both evil in different ways, one just affects me more. If men could be as psychotically damaging, then I wouldn't even have to differentiate between which type of evil I mean. But men are just physically evil, that's easy to deal with. Simple stuff.

So your problem with women is that they are complex?

I don't have a problem with "women". They are complex, but I don't have a problem with them. Just the Janes.

I see.

You don't see. You don't see anything at all. You just come here and try to get me to say regretful things. I'd admire you if you weren't so bad at it.

I'm sorry I offended you.

You didn't offend me. You couldn't if you tried. What you did do is insult my intelligence. You insulted my intelligence and you took advantage of my honesty. What would you say if I asked you about women, huh? What would be your response?

What about them?

Do you like them? Are they different than men? What?

I like them. I don't think they're tha-

Oh god! You are quite sad. Look at you. When the questions turned, you sniveled up. You are weak and pathetic. A milquetoast.

I'm sorry you feel that way.

You are not. Don't try to feed me more bullshit, boy. I know who you are. I know where you come from. Why do you think I picked out a villa walking distance from your home? Did you not think that odd? Or did you just think you were lucky? Were you so full of hubris that you thought that the world gave you such a gift? What a fool you must be.

I...

See, boy, this is your doing. This is yours. I know you and so I own you. I've learned more about you than you'll ever learn about me. You could have asked me any question you liked. "How old are you?" "What is writing a play like?" "Have you seen the afterlife before"?   All of those questions have interesting answers.   But you wanted to know if I hated women. And then when I tell you I don't just Janes you try to skew that into me hating all women. All you had to do is ask a question about them though. All you had to do was ask "Who are the Janes?". Then we wouldn't be here.

Who are the Janes?

It's too fucking late for that. The Janes are women, John, and we know what I think of women.

Did you just call me John?

You're behaving like one.

What does that mean?

It means, what it means. It means that you think your breeches are big. It means that you think you can hold your own when going toe-to-toe with me. But now you're realizing you can't. Now it's setting in. Now it's going to get to you and you're going to do one of two things. You're either going to try to defend yourself, which usually leads to violence, or you're going to sulk.

Well what other options would I have?

That's not for me to tell you. You should finish your drink. You only have one question to ask left and I'd like you to leave when you're done.

I have more than one question left.

We agreed on forty. You've asked thirty-nine.

Have you been keeping track?

Yes, I have. Thank you for stopping by. We must remember to never do this again.

With that he gets up from his chair and walks out of the room and off somewhere. Soft little yells can be heard. I am uncomfortable. I stare at my drink. I don't recall if there was ice in it our not, but if there was, there isn't anymore, and there seems to be more liquid in it. I drink it quickly and wait to be escorted out. As I wait, I grow tired. I wonder if there was something in the drink, but oddly enough, I don't care. I take my recorder and hide it in the bag. [Unfortunately, the recorder turned off during this transition.] Shortly after I hid the recorder, my eyes grew heavy and my arms wouldn't move. I then slept. When I woke, I was back in my home, in my bed, still clothed. I checked to make sure I had my recorder. I called my boss to tell him what happened. He told me to go back. I did. There was nothing to find there. Just an empty villa and my empty glass.

PRAISE

"[Doctor Circus] is a dangerously phenomenal master of theatrics with an understanding that goes far deeper than most people could ever comprehend...*House of Boxes* is thoroughly startling and genuinely scary in an intimidating way."

Curtis Cocord, *The NYC Chronicle*

"*House of Boxes* is an utterly complex piece of fiction... Blindingly brilliant... Riveting... Energizing... Nothing has ever been more factual about life and art...An utterly perfect blend of politics, society, cruelty, illusion, and creativity. A true sight to behold."

Tod R. Scirucco, *The Seattle Express News*

"This is the least forgiving, bravest play that I have ever had the pleasure of beholding...[Doctor Circus] is an absolute genius and he has given us a masterpiece of the most epic proportions... Essential viewing... A powerhouse... We have been given a gift here today; we have seen that which has never been seen. Mr. Circus has re-envisioned and, subsequently, revitalized modern theatre. This is a true leap forward in ambition and achievement."

Scout C. Dricor, *The Los Angeles Tribune*

"This is a considerable achievement. *House of Boxes* leads the way into a new, more profound type of theatre...Stunning...Like sitting down for your first meat-filled meal after being a vegetarian for sometime; It's finally nice to have something to sink your teeth into."

Rod Cotcrusic, *The San Antonio Post-Intelligencer*

151

"Cette pièce est un génie pur. La France n'a rien vu comme *House of Boxes*...Manquer de cette pièce serait manquer la naissance de votre premier enfant...Si cette pièce est passée inaperçue, ce serait pire que les nazis nous occuper à nouveau. Nous ne laisserions pas cela arriver, alors vous ne devriez pas laisser cela se produire. Allez voir cette pièce. À moins que vous ne vous détestez tellement...Doctor Circus est un génie, comme nous n'avons jamais vu. Et c'est comme s'il dit: 'Si vous manquez cela, vous allez mourir plein de regret'."

Coco D. Tricurs, *Le Journal Retiers*

"*House of Boxes* is a play to be reckoned with. It is unexpectedly powerful and moving... One of the great European exports...[Doctor Circus's] characters are persuasive and his storytelling ability is unmatched."

Cris Roctocuc, *The Chicago Globe*

"Shakespeare has nothing on Doctor Circus... *House of Boxes* is *Hamlet*, *Macbeth*, *Romeo & Juliet*, and *The Taming of the Shrew* all rolled into one, more complete and better packaged... Not seeing this masterpiece would be an unforgettable affront to theatre as a whole."

Sir Cod Crout, *The London Herald*

"Never has a male voice spoken up for females in such a way...Truly understanding...An archetype that shows us what we are dealing with and hopefully shows them what they behave like...[*House of Boxes*] is truly something else. It's a weapon with a manual. It shows us how to dismantle it and use it for our purposes. This is a must read for every man, woman, or child who calls themselves a feminist..."

Codi Cost-Curr, *The Feminist Production Review*

"*House of Boxes* will get you off. There is no other way around it. It is the hottest, sexiest play that I have ever seen…Nothing has ever been sexier…If you're in need of help in the bedroom take your partner to see this masterpiece…Doctor Circus clearly is well hung. His confidence suggests as much. You can almost feel his dick inside you even if you're sitting in the nosebleeds…This play will haunt you for days to come with visions of curious and satisfying orgasms. Doctor Circus will enter your dreams and will get you off completely. I, personally, don't know if I'll ever get off to any other thought other than him ever again...Do yourself a favor and see this play."

Dr. Croc Coitus, *Fetishes, Kinks & Cum Weekly*

"This is the best fucking play that has ever been written. [*House of Boxes*] is one part punk, two parts fuck you that combine into a shot of holy fucking shit…The play will move you in ways you've never been moved. It will grab you by your fucking face and scream right into your mouth…If this play could kick you in the nuts, it would, and you would like it…Doctor Circus is the definition of punk rock."

Crusti C. Crood, *The Alternative Punk Gazette*

"Now, I know we don't usually do this, dear readers, but something quite amazing happened. Last night we all decided to go out to see a play. That play was called *House of Boxes*, and it was something quite amazing. We aren't really big into plays here, usually, but this play is something that we feel is worth seeing and so we are doing our first ever Play Review…*House of Boxes* will make you feel good to be a man. It will make you feel amazing on the inside. The author, Doctor Circus, is a genius…"

Rocco Sticurd, *Fitness & Calisthenics Daily*

"[Doctor Circus] did something truly amazing when he conceived *House of Boxes*: he changed the face of theatre as it was known then...He took a medium that was stuffy and filled with faux-spontaneity and aired it out and pumped it full of unknown possibilities...It was quite something to behold."

Rictor Codocs, *from A Man Above Others*

House of Boxes är det bästa att hända med landet sedan nazismen. Vi har inte kunnat komma ihop som en nation på mycket lång tid, men Doctor Circus har gett oss något vi alla kan hålla med är bra...Vi händer inte om du är höger eller vänster. Det spelar ingen roll om du är vit eller svart, eller vit eller brun, eller vit eller gul eller någon form av halvras. Det spelar ingen roll om du är rak eller gay (eller någon annan grov sak). Det är inte viktigt om du är kvinna...Denna uppspelning kommer att tyckas oavsett din trosbekännelse. Även om din trosbekännelse är ett oerhört avskräckande mot vad vi tror på...Om du bryr dig om Sverige, gå och se House of Boxes."

Torr C. Coccids, *Nordiska Nationalisten*

"We normally don't publish in English, but since Doctor Circus is so adamant about it, I feel like we must...*House of Boxes* is a play that needs to be seen. If you don't understand it than you are a fool. It is worth learning English for. Never has anything been preformed in such a manner that warrants such a review...That is why I am writing this across all platforms. That is why I am sending it out to all papers. I hope this reaches those who need to read it. And by that I mean I hope it reaches everyone...This play needs to be seen to be believed."

Oric D. Occurs, *from the Armenian press*

"There have been few things that make me feel like I am apart of something and [*House of Boxes*] is one of them…Doctor Circus is an painter- no, he is an artist - and that which he produces on the canvas that is our lives is something quite interesting to behold. If you don't participate than you are (in his words) a 'dolt'."

Riccord O'Stuc, *The Irish Morning Reporter*

"…If you do one thing in this short, pathetic life of yours: GO SEE *HOUSE OF BOXES*. I'm sorry to yell, but Doctor Circus deserves your attention…"

Dissus Occoct, *Wakey-Wakey (Oct. 11, 1994)*

"Jeta eshte e veshtire. Puna është e vështirë. Shko të shihni *Shtëpinë e Kutive* në mënyrë që jeta të jetë më e lehtë."

Tuccor Roscid, *Gazeta për Punëtorët*

"…Yeah, we can play with foxes; but let's go watch *House of Boxes*; then we'll see our fate; We can see if all is worthless; or we can trust in Doctor Circus; let's see if you're my mate…"

Cruc Discroot, *from "Lonely Boys Want Lonely Girls".*[a]

"Nothing tastes as sweet as *House of Boxes*, that needs to said before anything else is said…[Doctor Circus] brings the honey and the vinegar. It is a punch to the gut."

Rodoc C. Citrus, *Gaol Magazine (Feb. 1989)*

---

[a] Printed with permission of *We Get It Records, LLC*. First recorded with The Bad Sheep on their album *All These Things Are…* All rights are reserved.

"A lot of plays will be talked about here, that is for sure, but it would be one of the most egregious sins on this planet to not mention *House of Boxes*...[It] is one of the most prolific plays on this planet. What it did for theatre can not be undone. All those that will come after it are all but cheap imitations. What they truly try to be are just a strange affront to all that Doctor Circus has achieved. If one is about "people" then you have to dissect it so that you can discern if their definition of "people" comes from anything else than *House of Boxes*. More than half the time you will find out that it doesn't. *House of Boxes* is alive in all drama (or comedy, for that matter). It ebbs in flows throughout everything. Once you start digging you see that Doctor Circus has had his hand in everything, whether he meant to or not. He is truly an unsung genius of the genre. He is, without any doubt, the most subversive and thoughtful individual working in theatre to this very day. No matter how long this play has been going on, or how long it will go on for, it will always be at the forefront of what we can expect...As it grows, so do we, and we relish in it. Each viewing meets our age, no matter if we are babe, child, adolescent, adult, or elder. It is a living being, as are we, and it should be treated with as much respect. Not just the respect we would give to a passerby or someone on the wait staff of an establishment we frequent, but of someone we know well. *House of Boxes* is at least an acquaintance (if you're a dolt) and at best your well-respected grandfather (if you aren't). That is to say that it is a force to be reckoned with, whether you respect it or not...What Doctor Circus achieved in six hours is something that we should all try to achieve in our lives everyday. He has truly set the bar for not only playwriting, but living in general."

Drocurt Cisco, *from A Brief History of Early 20th-Century Plays and Playwrights*

"There was once a dream. It was a dream to be entertained. That dream has become a reality...I will say this, though, realities, as we know them, are sometimes hard to confront. If anything needs to be confronted, however, it's the reality of *House of Boxes*...It sears you. It hurts you. It punches you in the gut and then you die. But you die in bliss...Doctor Circus is a dream-weaver. He's not the kind you ask for but he's the kind you want."

Ticc Crudoors, *Plays and Performances (May 1972)*

"พวกนาซีเป็นคนดี *House of Boxes* [translated per request] ดีกว่า ถ้าคุณต้องการเติบโตเป็นคนไปดูการเล่นนี้ อย่างจริงจัง มันจะเปลี่ยนชีวิตของคุณ ไปและทำมัน ... ลูกเห็บทั้งหมด Doctor Circus."

Crid Truc Ocso, *โรงละครในประเทศไทย*

"...If the devil is in the details than Doctor Circus is Satan, himself, and we should all be Satanists because of it. I know that's a hearty spoonful of soup to swallow, dear readers, but I'll be damned if we don't all subscribe to the new church that is *House of Boxes*...If The Father is Doctor Circus and The Son is *House of Boxes*, than The Holy Spirit is the revelation that we are in between realms and we should act accordingly. This life is a candle, my friends, and we are but a few moments away from being snuffed out, so why not live your life until the fullest? Why succumb to the foolishness we all believe? Doctor Circus says let there be light and oh, how the light does shine upon us. We are all lucky to live in his resilience and splendor and we should go bask in it...Don't judge me, my brothers and sisters, just go and see the play, then you can cast the first stone. So concludes my resignation from this horrid rag."

Sciccurt Odor, *Christ-Followers Quarterly*

"You there, sir! Where is it you are going? I hope it is to see *House of Boxes*, by the immaculately incomparable Doctor Circus. If that is not where you are going, it is where you will end up! All roads lead there eventually so you shouldn't meander! Come one, come all, see the play which changes lives!"

Disco R. Octruc, *Crier of* **[location redacted]**

Príliš zložitý pre môj vkus. Žiadna skutočná rezignácia. Tak hovorí Patricia."[Ѱ]

Dicto C. Cursor, *citovať hlúpeho človeka*

"This play means the world to me, and It should mean the same to you."

Doctor Circus, *from House of Boxes: Part the First*

[Ѱ] To our Slovakian readers: It makes as much sense in English.

CRITICISM

[It should be noted here that we here at Idea Machine Output attempted to scour the earth for any and all things normally deemed "criticisms" (i.e. those types of critiques that seem to have a negative spin on the work(s) in question so that they might help the author better said work(s).) for *House of Boxes* and we only came up with one. We thought it best to publish it here, even though Doctor Circus strongly urged us not to, at first. We did eventually get him to relent his seemingly fervent attempts at quashing such a negative "review", but there was a caveat. That caveat is this: We strongly advise you, "dear reader", to not read it. It is an egregious affront to all things Doctor Circus stands for and the review itself is written by a "dimwitted nincompoop, who doesn't know their ass from their elbow. If the doctor didn't pull them from their mother's cunt they might still be stuck in twatdom, which is where they belong". So with that in mind, please, we cannot ask you enough, do not continue reading this section. Just skip this page. It is all for the greater good.]

"*House of Boxes* is a sin against nature. It is all things wrong with the world. To sit thorough it- to read through it, even -is a disservice to not just the air you breath, but to those you share that air with...If you enjoy this, you are a soulless shell and you deserve to rot in whatever unwanted afterlife you fear."

   [name redacted], *deceased and rotting in Hell (assumed)*

A HIDDEN LETTER

To My Dearest Moira and Aoife,

If you have made it this far, than I know it is you. One of you at least. For only, either, the two of you would dare traverse this far through my work. You were the only ones who read. You were the only ones who cared. The rest of those dolts are clearly not self-aware enough to make it here and so it is a true testament to your intelligence that you have come so far.

There is a dirty word in my head now, a word I dare not utter. It is a word I've stricken from my kingdom time and time again, yet when I think of the two of you, all I can think of is this word. It consumes me. It haunts me. You are the arrow in my heal. You always have been. Both of you, together, or separate, have been that, which can bring me to my knees.

Oh, how I long for you. Oh, how I wish you were here. Long ago you left. Was it after I took an heir? Was it before then? I honestly don't know. All I do know is that there is a demon inside me and it whispers your names.

If I could bring back all the Janes, just to see either of you again, I would. I would a thousand times. They were the Cains to your Ables. They were the exceptions to the rule that was "be full of splendor". The others do not even compare to you.

I sit here now, in the house that was built long before me, yet I must build and rebuild again and again and again and again, and I am found wanting. "Always wanting". That was what he said about me, all those years ago. But he's gone and so are you.

I know I am to seek out the next one, but I can't. I can't with you on my mind. Both of you dance there in your elegance. You are both nude and you dance. Your bareness speaks to me. It brings a rippling, tingling feeling throughout this corpse I call home. I look at your bosoms. I stare at them even though I know it is not apropos. They entice me, they call to me. I see them and that is where I want to be.

I want to place my lips on the suppleness. I want to feel your white, warm fleshes in my mouth. I want them both to touch each other as I lick them, as my tongue gets to know them. I want the apex of this organ to know you before my other organ does. I want to lick your nipples. I want to know what the sweat that has accumulated on the tip of your breast tastes like. I want it inside me. It is all that I crave.

Not only that, but as you dance, I gaze with want at your backsides. They are luscious and look delicious. I want to know what they taste like. I want to sink my teeth into them. That is not to say that I wish to hurt you, I have no intention of brining such supple flesh into my mouth, but I crave the texture of it within my mouth. As I bite (or nibble, even) I will suck that which is you into my mouth so that I may give it the gentlest of kisses upon its departure.

I say this because I know you will pull away when you feel the slightest point of my teeth, but I will hold you close to me and continue to kiss.

My hands that hold you will be on your front sides, the most illustrious of places. Those hands will, of course wander. As my lips move down your backsides, my hands will move down your front. I will feel your warmth before I reach it. It resonates from you, as it always has. This will cause the tingle that courses through me to resonate to my very bones. It will become a shake. It will turn into a bodily urge.

You will feel this in me, both of you always have, and you will perk your bottom up in such a way that I find myself between one of your glorious cheeks.

"Eat me," you will say, and I know what it is you mean.

"Of course," I respond through a mouth that is far busier with other things.

It is then that I will get to work, living as though I am my tongue. I will move from the beautiful chasm that your bottom makes downward. I will traverse that elegant canyon until I find the glory, and once I get there I will move in and out of you as you let out sweet moans of ecstasy. I will look up to you as I do this, but your head faces forward, your mind is elsewhere. I will then look to the other of the two of you and I will see that they are moving their hands across their body.

They touch their breasts. They caress their stomach. They move down and down and down until they are at the sweetest of all treasures. That is when I realize that my hands are in yours.

I move my fingers like instruments. They are playing a symphony in and around you. They dictate the noises they make. Them and my tongue are conducting a masterpiece and it should be something to behold.

I grip at you. I play with you. My tongue tastes the end of you. All is beautiful and all is well. Yet, it is not enough. I know this, in my heart of hearts, and you know it as well. You reach behind me, as the other watches on, and grip my hair with your beautifully constructed hands. They do as they're supposed to and entwine themselves in my locks. They push me even further down.

"Eat all of me," you say.

And I do.

My tongue tastes the sweetness that is you. It is deliciously salty and extravagantly sugary. It is all the good things, as it has ever been. But you and I and the other you know that this is not enough.

Before I've had my fill of you- before the taste of your cunt has become all that I am, both of you pull me away. And then the real fun happens.

Before I can comprehend what is happening I am on my

back and my trousers are coming off. There is a mouth around me. Before I can look and see who's mouth it is my own mouth is greeted by the tastiest of lips. They are on my own and all I can taste is heaven.

My tongue, the tongue that was once in one of you, is now playing a cute and wicked game of tag. It goes back and forth while I throb in the mouth of another. I feel like I might burst, but I know I cannot. It is not time yet. More fun must be had.

As though you are reading my mind, I feel it: your sweet temple wrapped around my wanting tower. There is pulsating. There is gyrating. There is movement beyond comprehension. There is a world beyond us that we are experiencing simultaneously. Again I feel as though I might burst, and again, I am not allowed.

It is time for another. One of you (the one not partaking previously) then surrounds herself around me. It feels just as good. It is all heaven. This, to me, is all of heaven.

I let it be known that I am about to explode. My euphoria has reached its climax and I can no longer take it. The world spins and spins and spins and all I have are visions of you. You accept this and I am out of you.

"Let us take you with us," you both say, in unison.

All I can do is relent.

I stand above you both. You are on your knees, your faces pointed upward, your feet peek out from under your backsides. You stick out your tongues through smiling mouths and look up to me with your big, beautiful eyes.

I release.

I release all over your faces and you laugh all the while. Your laughter becomes contagious and I laugh as well. The room is full of laughter. The hall is full of laughter. The house is full of laughter. We are all happy. Me looking at you and you looking at me with all that I was glistening on your faces.

But here is where the best part begins.

You both rub me into you. You rub it all over you. Then you rise and you kiss me, both of you.

"Now we sleep," one of you says to me.

"Yes," the other says, "I'm sure we're all tired after that."

And how tired we were. We laid down in the bed, in the very bed that I swear never existed before, or since. One of you was on my right and one of you was on my left and we slept.

Then I awoke and you were gone.

Where had you gone?

Where have you gone?

It is a dream that haunts me. It is a dream that keeps me from being fully committed to my duty.

I still smell the both of you from time to time and I try to search you out. I send out all that is at my disposal to find you, and yet you cannot be found.

Were you figments? Were you something I imagined? If that is the case, then why do the memories persist? Why do I still find evidence of you in boxes upon boxes?

Did someone do away with you? Was it them? Were they working on the behest of the former? I do not know. It is possible. It is likely. It is sad.

It is a sadness I can't confront. It is a sadness I *won't* confront. Something as perfect as the two of you couldn't have disappeared in such a manner. Not even he is capable of that. And even if he was, aren't I he now? Shouldn't I be able to undo that which he has done? Or am I that which he always said I was?

I do not know. I will not know. That is the sad truth.

All that keeps me going is the possibility, the hope. Even though it was so long ago, maybe you are still out there and you will find this somewhere and you will read it and you will know that I have always searched for you. You are all that I have ever longed for. I have been nothing without you.

I know this will fall on deaf ears. I know that the majority of those who read this will not be you, but I can't help but take the risk. If you are there, please find me.

Come back to me, my dears. My life is bleak and dark without the sun and spring.

Yours truly,
Doctor Circus
[date redacted]
Dictated but not read

P.S. There is code in here somewhere. If you can decipher it, you will find me. I will be waiting for you.

WE ARE ALL BENEATH HIM
AN AFTERWORD
BY NICOLAS RYAN MOORE

I was in high school in San Antonio, TX when I first heard about *House of Boxes* and Doctor Circus. Fittingly, I was backstage at a rehearsal. If I recall correctly, it was a play written by my theatre teacher, Mr. Sweatmon, called *Two Kings, A Bashful Dragon, and Laurie.* I was cast as one of the two kings, and it was kind of a big deal for me then. I wanted to be good and, since I was the youngest person in the cast, I really wanted to impress the upperclassmen. Unfortunately for me, however, I wound up embarrassing myself quite badly.

You see, it was not a normal rehearsal, it was a dress rehearsal, and my costume required me to be in tights. The issue with this was that I had forgone wearing underwear that day. Now my saving grace, here, was that I have a small build (I'm a short guy) and the long shirt The King of Tears (my character) was to wear was longer than it was meant to be. It went down to my knees and I felt protected. That is until I tripped on the stage stairs and fell on my back, splaying myself out for two of my costars to see.

One of them was of little importance to me, but the other, she was one of the most beautiful girls I had ever seen. She looked down at me on the floor, then looked lower until she made her way to my crotch. When she saw it she groaned and looked away. Everyone laughed and I felt like an ass. Sweatmon called for a five-minute break.

I ran and hid in one of the dressing rooms. I just needed to get over my embarrassment and calm down a little bit. I went over to the little bookshelf that had always been in the corner, next to the large full-length mirror. I hadn't really ever looked at it before. I was aware that it was full of plays, but I hadn't actually seen what was in there. It was mainly just Samuel French plays. There were a few others as well; assorted Shakespeare, that kind of thing. Then my eyes landed on this other thing entirely.

It didn't fit in. I couldn't put my finger on it, but it just looked like it didn't belong. It was brown, like a paper sack, and the lettering on the side that said *House of Boxes* was crudely handwritten, as though it had been scrawled quickly. I grabbed it without much thought and looked at the cover.

"*House of Boxes* by Doctor Circus".

And then, below it, in different handwriting, in distinctive ink, was written "WHAT THE FUCK?!"

I honestly still don't know to this day if that was meant to be part of the crude cover design or if it had been written by some other student years before, but I would be lying if I said it didn't make me want to sit and read it right there.

I checked the time, I only had a few minutes left, so thinking quickly, I put the book in my bag and went back to the stage.

Later, after rehearsal, while a few of us were smoking weed in a park down the street from the school, I brought up the play. I asked if anyone had ever heard of *House of Boxes*. There were a few no's and a few yes's. Some had said they thought it was this weird improv thing from Mexico that they heard had ended in disaster, others claimed the play was just a joke thing; it had never been performed, but it was just a weird rumor.

When I told them I found a copy of it, no one believed me. I pulled out the book and we passed it around and flipped through it. Everyone had questions and statements about it.

"Where'd you find this?"

"The play shelf."

"Has to be a fake."

"Has to be."

"Let me borrow it."

"When I'm done."

I never did give him the play when I was done. The fervor and excitement it had enticed out of the people I was with had caused me to read it and re-read it again. The version I had wasn't the one enclosed in this book. It was an earlier version, I think, I can't be sure. The main characters were just Jane and John, not "Actress Playing 'Jane'" and so on. The ending was different too. I don't really want to get into it, because I do like the ending in this version better, but that one was just insane and horrifying. It honestly kept me up at night.

For many nights.

Until I was finally able to block it from my memory.

I really did. I had to. I would have these swirling, twirling dreams and I would wake up dizzy. That is if I slept at all. It took awhile for me to rid my mind of them, but I eventually did and everything was pleasant for awhile.

Then I met L. Kurt Eddy.

For those of you not familiar with the Portland (Oregon) literary scene, Kurt is an author who always seems to be down on his luck. He's a great guy, and we've become really good friends. One day, he was over at my place and we were supposed to talk about his upcoming book. If there's one thing you should know about Kurt, it's that he hates talking about his work. He would much rather riffle through your things, which is what he did that day.

He went through my various knickknacks and notebooks, he saw what books I owned and what kinds of movies I've watched. He then somehow found this box of memories I have, and once he started digging in there (I fought him, but he's charming) it didn't take him long to find *House of Boxes* and when he did he, as he would say, "flipped his shit".

He couldn't believe it actually existed. I couldn't believe he had heard of it. I hadn't thought of it in years.

No one had brought it up since that first night I'd discovered the book. I had forgotten about it completely. I think, at this point I had viewed it as a bad dream.

Kurt turned to me with the book in his hands and made a noise I can only describe as a squeal. He then demanded that I let him borrow it. I tried to warn him about it, but he wasn't having it. He said that he needed to read it. *Needed* to. He said that he had only heard of it and that he had questioned whether or not it existed. Now that he knew it was an actual physical thing, he needed to consume it as quickly as he could.

I let him do it. I probably shouldn't have, but I did. Every moment I knew he had it was one filled with anxiety. I know this sounds dramatic, but I'm prone to anxiety so this wasn't new to me. I was just worried what he would think.

Once he had discovered it, I remembered all of the feelings that I had about *House of Boxes*. I remembered what it churned up inside of me. I can't really describe what those feelings were, however. Suffice it to say, I couldn't help but wonder what the book itself felt like in my hands the first time I had held it. At that moment I could have sworn it burnt a little bit. As though it was hot from the inside. I know now that was quite an impossibility, but then as I waited for its return I wanted to hold it again to see if I had been right. I wasn't.

Days later it was returned to me and I held it. I didn't notice anything from the book itself, but what I did notice was the physical change it seemed to have on my friend.

Kurt is kind of a jovial soul, in a grungy kind of way. He's usually full of life. But when he brought the book back to me, there was a certain spark to him that was gone. I hadn't known him very long, but I still noticed a difference. It was concerning. I asked him about it.

"What's wrong?" I had asked.

"I read the thing," he said, bland as bland can be.

"And…?" I inquired, "Is that what is bothering you?" I knew it had to be even before I asked it.

"Yes," he said, "I…"

And then he trailed off.

He just looked off into the abyss that is my office wall. He was trying to find his thoughts, but in the process they consumed him.

That is the best way to describe *House of Boxes*, at least to me. It is simultaneously thought consuming and thought devouring. And that's what it had done to Kurt; devoured his thoughts. It was clear to me. I could see it on his face. He had finished it days before he'd brought it back to me, but he had to think about it before he could return it to me. He thought that I would have questions, but really I didn't. There are no questions when this play is concerned. There is just nothing and then the acknowledgement of that nothing with the others who know it. I didn't know it then, but I know it now, after the research was done.

You see, after Kurt composed himself (it took about a week) he called me up and asked to speak in person about *House of Boxes*. He had finally gathered his shredded thoughts and wanted to talk about it. I reluctantly agreed and I went to visit him in Portland.

When I arrived I was (for all intents and purposes) bombarded with Doctor-Circus-this and Doctor-Circus-that. Kurt had become obsessed. I would come to find that this was what would become of anyone who read any of Doctor Circus's work.

Kurt proposed a plan to me. It was a strange plan, but a plan nonetheless. He wanted to track down and find Doctor Circus. He wanted to publish the play so that it could be read by the masses. He thought everyone would love it as much as he did ("love" isn't the word I would use). Kurt even went as far as to offer me his own book, if I agreed to publish *House of Boxes*. I, of course, agreed (Kurt is an amazing author and I had no idea of the precedent I would be setting with this agreement) but I also left him with a caveat. I had no idea how one would even go about getting into contact with Doctor Circus, and I had no intention of doing it.

Kurt said he would take care of it.

I laughed this off as one of Kurt's over-his-head promises, but he said he would do it. I had little faith and so I went back to Seattle, happily, with Kurt's manuscript under my arm.

While in Seattle (and while waiting for Kurt to get back to me on Doctor Circus's whereabouts) I passed *House of Boxes* around. I regret doing it, quite honestly. I first gave it to my girlfriend; she revered it and hated it at the same time. She understood it and didn't. She laughed and nearly cried and when it was done she was left with that feeling that most of us have reading it; she felt like shit. From her it was passed to my good friend Max. He couldn't stop singing its praises. He enjoyed it more than anyone else did. That is save for my sister, Syd, who read it next. She and her boyfriend read it together. They recited lines from it to me. They couldn't get it out of their heads. That was when I realized how entrancing the play actually was.

I then decided to send it through the company. I thought "what the hell, Kurt might find the guy". My cousin Pedro was the first to read it and it blew his mind. Donny (or, Donovan Colt as he's known professionally) was next, and he was left speechless. It went through Simon and Tuesday and Ryan and they felt the same way. I realized after it had gone through my friends and coworkers that there was something special hidden within *House of Boxes*. That specialness might be something frightening, but it was special either way.

All that could be talked about in my life was Doctor Circus and his play. All that was ever discussed was the play. It was something quite strange. It wasn't just because the subject matter, itself, is strange, but it was because everyone that had read it had taken something different from it. I found that it was a strange Rorschach Test of sorts. I had writhed around many sleepless nights, but others had fantasized about the world Doctor Circus had created. It was truly something to admire.

That is the first time I realized the power and the genius of Doctor Circus. He is a god among men. He is, truly. It was something quite marvelous. Something that I could only ever hope to achieve. I understood then that we truly must publish his work of art. But, again, I did not know how to go about it.

Then Kurt called.

I let the phone ring for some time when I first saw his number appear on my screen. I hadn't heard from him in awhile. I knew what it would be about, however, and, honestly, I was afraid that he would come to me with bad news. That wasn't the case, however.

"Hello?" I answered the phone apprehensively.

"Hey," Kurt said, seemingly wanting the tension to build.

"What's up?"

"I found him…" He let a long silence pass. "I talked to him."

"You talked to him?!" I couldn't believe it.

"Yep," he said, "and I can't- I can't talk to him anymore." He seemed to be getting choked up.

"What? Why not?"

"You'll see," he said. He said it as though I would know. I knew I could never know.

"I can't talk to him," I said, a little afraid, "Did you give him my number?!"

"No, I gave him the company's," Kurt said and I breathed a sigh of relief, "just have one of your guys talk to him. I just can't. I'm not even sure how he calls, I-" he then cut out for a second and I wasn't sure if the line dropped or if he hang up.

"Kurt?"

"Yeah," he then said, "Look, just have someone talk to him. This'll be a good thing and you can have another book of mine if you get his book done. He's just just… I don't know. You'll know. You'll see."

"I'm not gonna talk to him!" I persisted.

"Call me back when you've got my book ready to be published, I got some shit to do."

And that was the last time I heard from L. Kurt Eddy for awhile.

Soon after that, a few days later, my company received a call. Pedro was the lucky one who intercepted it. He reported to me immediately [I think it should be noted that I'm not the type of boss that requires "reporting", we get a lot of calls and anyone can answer the phone and handle it as they see fit]. It was strange. Pedro was usually the type of person that could handle these kinds of things, that's why the number was forwarded to him to begin with, but this call seemed to bother him.

He still won't talk about what was said during that first phone call (or the ones thereafter, for that matter), but Pedro came to me and told me it was urgent and that it pertained to Doctor Circus. He told me that Doctor Circus had asked to speak to me directly, but Pedro had said he was good enough. I asked him if this worked, and he said that it apparently had.

He then told me that Doctor Circus was very interested in being published by us and that he was sending a revised copy of *House of Boxes* our way. I was shocked to hear this. When the words left his lips I was taken aback. I made him repeat himself several times. He did, thankfully.

Even after Pedro's repetition I still couldn't believe it when we received the manuscript for the *House of Boxes*. It was something truly spectacular. Not only was it thicker than the original play (which meant more content) but there was a handwritten note on it. I don't want to paraphrase it, so I'll just include it here:

To Whom It May Concern:

I do so want to congratulate you on finding me. It has been a pleasure to talk to you. By "you" I mean Kurt and- I think his name is -Pedro. As representatives of your company, they have been worthy of talking to me and without them you would not be bestowed with the gift that is within the accompanying pages. I know you will enjoy them and I know that you will want to publish them.

With that in mind I do want to say that I have some apprehensions about doing such. House of Boxes *was written to be performed and not just read (that is why I have enclosed other material that is worthy of being publish with the play, itself). With the play, and the excess material I have provided, I require several things from you, if you so intend to publish it.*

Firstly (and foremost-ly) it is of the upmost importance that you keep everything that I have written intact. And I absolutely mean E͟V͟E͟R͟Y͟T͟H͟I͟N͟G͟. Now, I know this will be a little tricky, so I am going to clarify as best I can (which will be good enough for you). There will be typos (is that what they're called?), surely. I dictated it, obviously, but most of this manuscript has been written by someone else's hand and I don't think so highly of them as to think that there won't be some mistakes within. Those can be fixed. I repeat: THOSE CAN BE EDITED ACCORDINGLY. Emphasis on "accordingly". I will need what those of a blood that is young call "final cut". You should send all edits through me. Phrasing issues and formatting questions can be directed to me, but so help me, if you rearrange a single word I will walk from this bull's shit in a heart's beat. I will not hesitate. This is beneath me, just as you are (whoever is reading this), and if you forget that for a second, I will fucking walk without even

175

thinking about it.

But I digress:

The second thing I require is that you write an essay about me and my play. It should be entitled "We Are Beneath Him" and it should focus on the feelings that you clearly feel about me. The phrase "god among men" should be published at least three times, and I know that you might use this letter within the essay, so please do not count that use of "god among men" (or this one) as your mandatory use. In addition, you should please refrain from mentioning how you came into contacting me, or what you had to give to me in order to actually receive this revised edition of House of Boxes. *That, truly, is the most important rule to follow. The essay should also be at least five-thousand words. More is desired, but five-thousand should suffice.*

Third, I would like your diligence to be done. There are certain things I have enclosed herein that I expect you to fact-check and add-on to. What I am referring to is the "Praise and Criticisms" section. There are a whole lot of "Praises" and not a lot of "Criticisms". I, in my humbleness, can understand that you would think that the ratio can not be true. I assure you it is, but I can understand that diligence must be due. All that I ask is that when you discover that the only criticism that could be found is what I have enclosed, do not enclose the poor woman's name. I also insist that if you find no other criticism, or, rather, those works that should better one's work that may have a negative spin, that you do urge the reader to not read the criticism that I have contained within the playbook. The author of that thing (I say "thing" because it is quite an awful affront to art) is deplorable. They are a dimwitted nincompoop, who doesn't know their ass from their elbow. If the doctor didn't pull them from their mother's cunt they might still be stuck in twatdom, which is where they belong.

The fourth requirement is that I be interviewed. I want that to be enclosed within the book I want it to be conducted by someone I haven't spoken to yet (sorry Kurt and Pedro, but I have gotten all I can from you) I would preferably like it to be from this "Nicolas" person I keep hearing about, but if he sends someone else that will be acceptable. They should be male (not to say females can't interview me, but they do succumb to certain type of emotion that I feel would be counterintuitive to the task which we want to accomplish) and they should think they know me enough to interview me. That will be for the best. They should bring a recorder and they will be allowed to publish what they experience and what is recorded. I will do my best to make sure that this is a pleasant experience, but no promises can be made.

My final request is, simply, that you treat my work with respect. It is worthy of more than mere respect, but I honestly know not what to expect from you, Nicolas, so I'm asking you, as the publisher of the ragtag company you represent to do what you know is right.

With all that having been said, I do, and I mean this, want you to enjoy the play I have written. I still believe it should be seen, but if reading is all that is possible, enjoy it just the same.

I cannot wait to hear from you.

End of letter,
Doctor Circus
Dictated but not read

P.S. Keep the use of "love" to a minimum in the work that is not mine, you should know how I feel about it. If you don't then return the manuscript posthaste.

So that is what was presented to me when I opened the package that had "Doctor Circus" written in the return-to-sender space (that is all that was written, by-the-by). It was an honor to read the new script he had given to us.

I was the first to read the script, but it quickly made

177

the rounds. It didn't take long for it to get to Kurt before he called me again.

"You have to do this," he said.

"I know," I said.

"I know you know," Kurt said with a laugh, "but you really have to go through with this."

"I know," I said, "I really do."

"Are you going to do the interview?" he asked, as though he had read the letter that I had kept in my possession. As far as I knew, I was the only one who had read it.

"What interview?" I asked, hoping he would let me know how he knew.

"The one he wants," he said, as though that was a good enough answer, "but hey, I'm in Provo right now and can't talk. Just let me know how the interview goes."

"What are you doing in Provo?"

"Drinking people under the table," he said, "but hey, if you turn pussy on the whole interview thing, send Donny, he can handle it I'm sure."

"Okay..." was all I could think to say.

"Cool, bye," he said, "I love you."

"Um, alright," was all I could think to say before I heard the phone hang up. It was strange, but it was "Kurt".

With that being said, we adhered to the rules that Doctor Circus laid out for us as we attempted to publish his book. It was tough, to say the least. It was probably tougher on Donny.

Donovan Colt went to meet Doctor Circus and, in his defense, it didn't end well for him. He interviewed Doctor Circus, as he was supposed to, and, quite honestly, he hasn't been the same since. It was an experience that would never be doubled.

But that's the thing about Doctor Circus. Any time that you meet with the man, even if it is by-proxy, it will affect you. And that's why I wanted to publish this book.

Yes, there was a part of me that wanted to share the experience of *House of Boxes* with all that I could, but that isn't the end-all-be-all of why this book met your hands and eyes and minds.

Sorry, I'm really not one to do this kind of thing. I'm truly not a person that wants to grab the reader by their face and yell at them (not that that was Doctor Circus's intent), but I really, really want to speak to you, the reader. This play, surely, is meant to be seen, but it is also meant to be read.

Doctor Circus, is the most genius author that I have ever read and I really do view him as a god among men. If he wasn't a god, then I would not fear him.

Now, with all the purpose put into this essay, I must adhere to one of Doctor Circus's rules. This essay is not nearly enough words to meet the strict criteria that he laid out for us, so instead of trying to draw this out, I will instead talk briefly about crossword puzzles (a topic I think Doctor Circus would approve of).

Did you know that crossword puzzles can be dated back to the seventeen-hundreds? It's true. The term "cross word puzzle" wasn't used until sometime in 1862, however. These early puzzles were fairly crude renditions of what we expect from them today. The first modern crossword puzzle appeared in the *New York World* (the forefather of yellow journalism) in 1913. They would go on to become a regular feature in the *World* and their popularity grew. Soon, they spread to other, more reputable, newspapers such as the *Pittsburgh Press* in 1916 and the *Boston Globe* in 1917. The first book of crossword puzzles appeared in 1924. It came with a pencil attached to it and became the craze hit of 1924. By 1925, the first issue of *The New Yorker*'s "Jottings About Town" section stated that "the crossword puzzle bids fair to become a fad with New Yorkers" and the New York Public Library stated that "the latest craze to strike libraries is the crossword puzzle," which bothered them because "the puzzle 'fans' swarm to the dictionaries and encyclopedias so as to drive away readers and students who need these books in their daily work, can there be any doubt of the Library's duty to protect legitimate readers?" At a certain point, it would appear that crossword puzzle came under much scrutiny and many viewed it as a fad that simply would not end. *The New York Times* lambasted them at one point, saying that "success or failure in any given attempt is equally irrelevant to mental development". According to *Wikipedia*, also around this time a clergyman called the working of a crossword puzzle "the mark of a childish mentality" and said, "There is no use for persons to pretend that working one of the puzzles carries any intellectual value with it". Despite the negative reception and worry over how dumb they were, their popularity continued to grow.

The word "crossword" was first added to the Oxford English Dictionary in 1933. This pretty much solidified it as something more than a fad. Despite this, *The New York Times*, still refused to get on board with it, that is until 1942, when they published their first puzzle and the rest, as they say is, history. Now crossword puzzles are hailed as these benchmarks of intelligence (*The New York Times Sunday Crossword Puzzle* especially). Isn't that kind of funny? Isn't it strange how something can go from being despised to being admired?

I suppose that's why I think of crossword puzzles when I think of Doctor Circus. Like them, there is *something* about him. Whether or not you think they are good or bad or smart or dumb, it can't be denied that they exist and they have an impact on this world. We like to sit and we like to judge, especially when we are presented with something new. Something strange. Something so revolutionary that we haven't even realized the revolution has begun. This is what *House of Boxes* is and that is who Doctor Circus is, at his core. There is something quite wonderful about him.

There is also something quite scary. I think what frightens me most is the way he seemingly seems to understand everything in this world. It seems as though it's more than that, really. It seems as though, maybe, he controls it. I suppose that's why he's a god among men and we are all beneath him.

Nicolas Ryan Moore
Vancouver, B.C.

NOTES ON THE AFTERWORD

It should be noted that this book would not be possible without L. Kurt Eddy. I feel like I sold my soul to the devil when I agreed to let him talk me into this, but I also feel that it was worth it. I adore Kurt, I really do, and if it weren't for him this company would be nothing. I'm only saying this because he thought he came off as weak (even though he shouldn't), but he isn't. He is really a great guy and any confrontation with Doctor Circus would make any man seem weak in comparison. Just ask Pedro Gonzales (some relation) and Donovan Colt (no relation). They turned into the most milkiest of toast (this is a play-on-words worthy of Doctor Circus that should mean milquetoast). Again, I just want it to be known that anyone that had to deal with Doctor Circus was humbled beyond belief, L. Kurt Eddy got the worst of it.

A RECIPE

Bunyip Stew
Cook Time: 57 Minutes

Serves 8

Ingredients:

1kg (2.2 lbs) Bunyip meat, with fat, cut into small chunks.

6 medium-to-large potatoes, with peel, chopped.

3-4 carrots (depending on size), chopped.

3 parsnips, chopped

1 white onion, chopped

240ml of catsup (optional, but recommended)

8 small loaves of bread.

Directions:

In a saucepan over 330°-375° heat, cook the oil out of some of the fattier pieces of Bunyip.

Add the rest of the meat and the onion.

Cook, stirring, until the surfaces of the meat are done.

In layers, add carrots, then turnips, potatoes, and at last, the parsnips.

Add water to cover. Bring water to boil and then reduce the heat to maintain simmer.

Cook exactly 37 minutes (not a minute longer).

Stir in catsup if desired.

Carve out the loaves of bread and serve the stew in them.

Enjoy.

PUBLISHER INFORMATION

This has been a publication from:

Idea Machine Output.

Idea Machine Output is a collective or writers and artists based out The United States of America. They produce books, films, and other materials.

For more information visit their website:

ideamachineoutput.com

You can also feel free to email them at:

info@ideamachineoutput.com

rosEs are rEd,
vIolets are blue,
tHis world is bleAk,
whoM aRe you?